FATHER *of* LIES

ANN TURNER

FATHER of LIES

An Imprint of HarperCollinsPublishers

HarperTeen is an imprint of HarperCollins Publishers.

Father of Lies
Copyright © 2011 by Ann Turner
www.harperteen.com
Library of Congress Cataloging-in-Publication Data
Turner, Ann Warren.
  Father of lies / by Ann Turner. — 1st ed.
    p. cm.
  Summary: In 1692, when a plague of accusations descends on
Salem Village in Massachusetts and witch-fever erupts, four-
teen-year-old Lidda, who has begun to experience visions and
hear voices, tries to expose the lies of the witch trials without
being hanged as a witch herself. Includes author's notes about
the Salem Witch Trials and bipolar disease.
  Includes bibliographical references.
  ISBN 978-0-06-137085-4
  [1. Manic-depressive illness—Fiction. 2. Trials
(Witchcraft)—Fiction. 3. Witchcraft—Fiction. 4. Salem
(Mass.)—History—Colonial period, ca. 1600–1775.] I. Title.
PZ7.T8535Fat 2011   2010015224
[Fic]—dc22   CIP
                                                       AC

Typography by Andrea Vandergrift
11 12 13 14 15   CG/RRDB   10 9 8 7 6 5 4 3 2 1
❖
First Edition

To my family, for their love, support,
and wise listening,
and to all those with bipolar disorder
who work so hard to make lives for themselves.

AUTHOR'S NOTE

The opinions about Native Americans expressed in this novel *only* reflect the historical record and not this author's beliefs. They are important to understanding this period. In Chapters Nineteen and Twenty-seven, some of the responses in the witch trials are taken directly from the historical transcripts of the trials.

1

THE FIRST TIME SHE SAW HIM WAS AT NIGHT as she lay in bed, with the wind tapping the maple branch against the pane. It was a cold January sound, and the fire Mama had banked in the big fireplace downstairs had long gone out. The chimney near the head of her bed radiated a small amount of heat, and her sister Susannah was curled tightly on her side of the bed, as if hoarding all the warmth.

As Lidda put her hand on the rough bricks, she caught a movement from the corner of her eye. The moon shone brightly through the window, illuminating the clothes chest against the wall. There. Something. Some*body*? Long and slim, upright and leaning against the wall as if it—he?—owned it.

"Nooo!" she whispered, pulling the covers over her

head. The Bible talked about temptations and "the Evil One," but it was Reverend Parris at church who most liked to frighten them, his face reddening, cheeks shaking with excitement as he thundered about what hell would be like, creating a fog of fear and terror, as if the whole village of Salem were surrounded by devils and evil spirits. Horrible man!

Now, despite the comfort of her bed, Lidda shivered, remembering, and cautiously poked her head partway out of the covers, giving a quick look toward the wall. Now he—*it?*— was sitting on the clothes chest, pressing his hands together, then out.

Torn between wanting to see more—after all, *she* was the brave one in the family, the one who rode Nell bareback into the woods, the one who stripped off her stays and danced under the green apple trees when no one could see—and the need to hide, Lidda kept her eyes just above the edge of the blanket.

The creature was looking at her. Its head turned with a swirl of long dark hair, and silver eyes gleamed in the moonlight like small stars. It seemed to be calling to her—

Lidda, Lidda, girl, do you see me? At last?

I have been waiting for you.

Because the voice was deep and inviting, Lidda thought it must belong to a he. She struggled not to answer.

With a gasp, she dove into darkness again and wiggled down as far as she could in the lumpy bed. Her sister stirred in her sleep and murmured. Lidda pressed closer to Susannah, taking comfort in her warmth. Suddenly she stiffened. What about dear Charity, asleep in her narrow bed nearby? What if this . . . thing, this nightmare made visible, frightened her younger sister?

I am not a nightmare, Lidda, and I am far more than a dream.

In the stuffy darkness, Lidda told herself, *He will go away, whatever he is—creature of the moon or of the night.*

When she woke in the morning, the top of the chest would be bare, the wall empty, and everyday life would resume once more. It must! Then a fierce and sudden heat swept up her body, making her want to heave off the covers, but she was afraid of waking Susannah.

PleaseGodpleaseGodpleaseGod, Lidda prayed. But God had no chance to answer her—or perhaps this was His answer—for Susannah woke up, cranky as usual and full of righteous words.

"Why are you waking me, sister? What is going on? Are you ill? You are hot and sweaty!"

She could never just say one sentence; it always had to be a bundle of complaints. Thrusting her head out and taking a deep breath, Lidda stuttered, "Nightmare, sister, a n-n-nightmare." She pulled away from Susannah to her side of the bed. Peering toward the chest, she saw the outline of the creature fading into the moonlight; first he was there, then a sketchy sense of his presence, then moonlight that had a kind of form and substance.

With a groan and another muttered complaint, Susannah subsided, and her breathing changed into the deep, rhythmic sounds of sleep.

Lidda did not sleep until the moon had set, just before the dawn. The figure seemed to have gone, but not his voice—not quite a whisper, or quite like a man's, but slow and sinuous as a winding river.

It is lonely here. . . .

I yearn for warmth . . .

. . . to be in a living being. . . .

She ducked her head under the covers, trying to shut

out the insinuating voice, which followed her down into the darkness.

I like your free spirit. . . .

I will be your friend. . . .

When she woke in the morning, those thoughts were still there, hovering over her mind like a dangerous river mist.

"Lidda!" Mama's voice echoed up the stairs the next morning. "Get dressed and come down to help with Thomas."

"Yes, Mama." She sat up. Charity's bed was empty, and Susannah was already gone. The blankets were twisted about her, as if she had thrashed and fought them all night long.

Standing on one leg on the cold floor, Lidda felt her head with both hands. It was touched by a presence of something not her own—a foreign, chilling touch. Frantically, she looked over at the chest where *he* had lounged as if he belonged there, as if he owned it.

Lidda whipped her head back. Nothing was there. She let out a sigh. It must have been her imagination. Her mother, when teaching her the alphabet long ago, had scolded her often about that. "Always dreaming,

5

Lidda! Pay attention to your letters so that you can learn to read, a privilege many girls would be happy to have!"

But her thoughts were not under her control. No one understood that, certainly not her mother. Ever since she had gotten her monthly courses last summer, at times her thoughts galloped away like unruly cows let out of their winter barn, kicking up their heels, dashing out of sight. She did not know how to call them back. No one did. They hurtled around inside her head, making her break out in a sweat or shout to the clouds overhead. One day last November she had even climbed to the top of the apple tree in back and leaped after a bird, hoping to touch its wings as it went by. She had crashed to the ground, luckily landing on a patch of soft moss, the only result of her wild daring a twisted ankle and a sore wrist.

"Lidda!" Mama's voice from below was definitely angry. It meant she would have extra chores to do if she did not get downstairs immediately.

Yanking a warm petticoat over her shift, then a brown skirt and bodice (she would not, would not, lace up her hated stays!), Lidda pulled on her stockings, thrust her feet into leather shoes, and dashed downstairs.

If she made a lot of fuss and noise, perhaps it would fool her mother into thinking she was paying attention and being busy. The sound of Thomas's wails beat on her ears as she ran into the kitchen.

An angular woman in a gray dress with wisps of hair escaping her cap looked up from the table where she was making bread.

"There you are." She sighed, clearly out of patience.

"Yes, Mama." Lidda bobbed a curtsy. "What do you want me to do first?"

Her mother pointed to the cradle near the fire, where her baby brother, Thomas—round faced, with black hair—howled and flailed his fists. At the table, Charity was chopping carrots for the noontime soup, and she gave Lidda a sympathetic glance, pursing her lips. The silent message was clear: *Be careful.*

But Susannah—red-haired Susannah of the perfect face and demeanor, the daughter Mama said they should all be like—sat on the bench, knitting stockings for the family. She did not look as if she ever saw anything strange or unnerving perched on their clothes chest at nighttime. If Lidda told her what she'd seen, her sixteen-year-old sister would click her teeth like an old lady and say, "For heaven's sake, Lidda, your imagination is like a runaway horse! Cannot you control it?"

No, I cannot, Lidda thought as she knelt beside the cradle and rocked it back and forth, singing. Her voice was high and clear, like the wind outside. It seemed to soothe her baby brother; his fists fell to his sides, the long eyelashes fanned against his cheeks, and his mouth slackened. Lidda sat back on her heels, satisfied. More than anyone else in the family, she could quiet Thomas and stuff those powerful wails back inside his body. It soothed her to be good at something in a family that constantly reminded her that she was dreamy, could not pay attention, and would probably never marry.

"What was happening last night, sister?" Susannah asked sharply.

"Last night?" Lidda assumed an innocent tone. *When he first came.*

"You woke me, kicking and burning up with heat! You should have felt her, Mama. No one could have slept through it!"

Her mother gave Lidda a quick, worried glance. "Are you well, daughter? Not sickening for anything?"

Lidda did not know how to reply; she wanted to say,

"Yes, Mama, I fear I am sickening for something. . . ." She paused and put one tentative finger against her cheek. And yet, and yet? That soft, inviting voice from last night, which told her that he knew her as no one else did . . . that he liked her free spirit . . . had anyone ever said that to her? And who *was* he?

"Perhaps you need a dose of my medicine, child," her mother said, turning back to the bread she was kneading. She dusted the planks with flour, slapped down the dough, and pushed it back and forth.

Lidda stopped rocking Thomas, fascinated by the motion, which caught at her thoughts.

Watch them go back and forth, like that grapevine I once saw the boys swinging on—they were having so much fun—I would like that—and once this dreadful snow is gone, I will take some rope from Papa and go out to a far tree, slinging it over a branch, and make a swing for myself, where I will go back and forth—

"Lidda!" Charity's voice finally pierced the racing flow of Lidda's thoughts. "What is wrong?"

She shook her head, murmured, "Nothing," and picked up Thomas to walk him about the perimeter of the room. It reminded her that she always *was* on the edges of things, on the margins. At least it was slightly warmer here than it was outside, where the deep snow erased all boundary lines and fences.

Back and forth echoed in her mind, and she brushed at her forehead with one hand. Oh, how she wished her mind were filled with snow, something cool and endless that would erase all of her thoughts, making a smooth sheet with no wrinkles, desperate hollows, or terrifying sights. Like that—creature—whatever he was, whoever he was.

Thomas reared his head back, giving her an intent look from his dark eyes. He seemed to know what she was going through, which was far more than *she* knew. She felt as if she had been cast adrift on a rushing river and could not reach out to grab a branch to stop herself. But then—but then—she had always vowed not to have a life like the other girls in the village; growing up under the thumbs of her parents, then marrying a husband who would take their place. And the babies would come, one, two, three, just like Mama's, but hopefully with none of them starting and not making it out into the light—the way the last two had—which had caused deep lines to be etched on her mother's face. . . .

At a gurgle from Thomas, Lidda stopped her pacing and looked at her family. *She* would not be like the other fourteen-year-old girls. She would do something bold, adventurous, and decidedly different. Perhaps she would run off and join the Wabanaki Indians farther north. Were they as cruel as the tales said? She thought people exaggerated, certain that the Indians did not make their children sit through hours of church services in a freezing building during winter, where you thought you might lose your senses from the unending boredom of the minister's drone. Yes, *she* was going to have an interesting life, somewhere far away from Salem Village. She just did not quite know how she would manage it.

The sibilant voice started up inside her.

I have come to help you, Lidda. You are already bold and adventurous—there was a hint of a laugh—*and you assuredly are different!*

"Who *are* you?" Lidda said aloud, startling her sisters and her mother, who took her hands off the bread dough and sent a piercing look at her daughter.

"Who is who, Lidda?"

"Ah, nothing, Mama . . . I—I am just remembering

Reverend Parris's last sermon, which was very frightening . . . about the Devil. . . ." She trailed off. It was the best she could do; she couldn't find another excuse.

Holding Thomas, Lidda squeezed him even tighter, pressing his warmth and solidity into her body. *What in heaven's name is happening to me?*

Heaven has nothing to do with this, girl.

2

"I KNOW, I KNOW, IT IS FREEZING COLD!"
Lidda's words were clipped and short, surprising as a
rattle of gravel on the windowpane.

"We only bathe once a month during the winter,
daughter!" Mama poked at the fire, sending new flames
shooting up the chimney. Thomas chortled from his
nearby cradle, holding out his hands to the light.

"I have to, Mama," Lidda insisted. "The water is
already hot. I will only use a little bit and put it in the
basin—if you can just make certain Papa and Jacob
are somewhere else, then I can wash by the fire."

"But, child—why?" Mama straightened, giving Lidda
an impatient look. "You never were one to insist on
bathing; that was more Susannah's idea."

From where she was sitting on the bench knitting a
long, gray sock, Susannah sniffed and said, "Just so—I

13

am the one who cares about cleanliness!"

Lidda sent a scathing look at the knitting in her sister's hands. *Gray isn't a clean color; it is ugly and meek. It does not even count as a color!*

"I'll help," Charity offered, bustling forward to swing the heavy iron pot on its hook directly over the fire. "I'll soap up your back, Lidda."

Ever since two nights ago, when Lidda had seared with heat beside Susannah in bed, Charity had become overly helpful, pulling up the covers last night so that only her sister's nose poked above, offering her own rag doll, Elizabeth, for company, "in case you wake up afraid at night."

Lidda had hugged her tightly, warmed by her sister's concern; she knew something was not right but did not seem to know what to do about it. Nor did she.

"All right, all right." Mama gave in. "You have helped all day with Thomas, and he has been a trial with his wailing and spitting up. My dress shall need a washing, too, Lidda." She gave her a weary smile as she took Thomas onto her lap and offered him her breast. She gasped as he bit down, stifling an involuntary yelp.

Lidda smiled. That boy had a lot of teeth. He would

14

be a toothsome boy. *Toothsome, sweet to the tooth, delightful as a pot of honey or a crisp apple in the fall.*

She went over to the table against the wall where they kept the things for washing up: a deep yellow pottery bowl, a brown wide-mouthed jug filled with homemade soap scented with Mama's lavender, and two faded woolen cloths used for washing.

Bringing the bowl and jug of soap over to the hearthstones, she set them down while Charity lifted the pot, pouring out the hot water in a steaming rush. Lidda's eyes strayed to the wet steam in the air—it would cover her face, wash her clean, and sluice through her head, taking away that new invading voice. Reverend Parris always droned on about cleanliness, the kind where one's soul is clean. *I do not know about my soul and how to get it clean, but at least I can have clean skin, legs, arms, and toes. And eyes and ears.*

Carefully she touched one finger to each ear, to her eyes, to her mouth, her chest, her stomach, each arm, and each leg. Her touch would make her safe. From *him.*

"Come, Susannah, help me hold up this sheet so Lidda can bathe behind it!" Mama commanded.

"But I am busy, Mother, you can see that. What I

am doing is far more important than my sister having a bath!" At a sharp look from her mother, Susannah flung down her knitting and stalked over to the fireplace.

Mama unfolded the sheet with a snap, handing one edge to Susannah, who lifted it reluctantly. "I do not see why you must do this, sister. After all, we had baths just last month. That is enough even for me!"

Lidda did not answer, tearing at her waistcoat, suddenly feeling that she might suffocate. She yanked her shift off over her head, unlaced her stays, ripped at the petticoats, and dropped them with her skirt on the floor. They made an ugly brown pool—ugly as the mud that came in spring. She could not seem to drag her gaze away from the floor and her thoughts of the slimy . . .

"Lidda?" Charity touched her lightly on one arm. "The bath?"

Apparently she was standing there completely naked, staring into the flames and mouthing something about . . . mud, for Susannah asked, "What is all this about mud?"

Mama chimed in, "It is months yet until it wells up on the Salem roads."

"Thank God for that!" Susannah exclaimed. "I far prefer this dry snow!"

Crouching beside the bowl of steaming water, Lidda watched Charity dip one of the cloths into the water, scoop soap out of the jar, and reach to scrub her back. It was almost like being brushed, as if she were their mare in the barn, being readied for an outing.

"Just like Nell! I'm being brushed!" Lidda chuckled, flinging out her arms, spraying all with drops of water.

"Careful!" Susannah yelped.

Again Lidda sprayed her with one arm flung wide; even a few drops scattered into her mama's surprised face. A look of dismay crossed her features and the sharp lines around her mouth and eyes. Then, suddenly, just as Lidda thought she would be scolded and punished, Mama laughed—surprising her.

"Water!" She held out her hands, her mouth struggling between dismay and laughter. "It is raining inside!"

Lidda sent a few more drops flying to her mother's hands, who patted them on her own creased cheeks and sighed, as if she were a patch of dry land suddenly blessed with rain. Charity beamed at them all, the forgotten cloth dripping onto the floor.

Then Lidda heard her father outside. "Hurry, hurry, Charity, Papa is coming!" Frantically she seized the cloth, rubbing it over her face, under her arms—with those strange bunches of hair that had sprung up last summer like unwanted clumps of grass—down her legs and feet, but never between her legs, for that would be too intimate, too embarrassing. With a last swab at her stomach, Lidda stood, grabbing the rough towel Charity held, scrubbing her skin briskly. She glowed. The inner voice was gone. She had washed him out. Her head was clean. Anything foreign or invasive had been brushed away.

Charity helped her pull on her clothes again, wrinkling her nose, as did Lidda, at the stale smell of the unwashed skirt and waistcoat. "We will wash them tomorrow, sister," she whispered, "and dry them on a line before the fire. Then you will be clean all over!"

Lidda seized her sister, pressing kisses on both plump cheeks, tugging on a wisp of blond hair that had escaped her cap. "Thank you, thank you," she said softly. Quickly, seeing her imprisoning stays on the floor, she kicked them under the washing table, hoping they would not be discovered.

"Now you will be better," Charity said. Crouching,

as if to pick some dirt off the floor, Charity retrieved the stays and tucked them beneath Lidda's cloak against the wall.

"Why would she need to be better?" said Susannah, folding up the sheet as Papa clomped into the room, shedding snow and cold air.

"What have we here? A bath in the coldest January we've ever seen? You must have lost your wits, all of you." Papa clapped his reddened hands together, and the odor of stables, manure, and cows floated out into the steamy room, which had—for a moment—smelled clean with the faint scent of lavender.

Jacob followed, knocking the snow from his boots and coming to stand, wide legged, by the fire. "Why, what in the world, Lidda?" He gazed at her solemnly, like some wise ancient instead of a seventeen-year-old with the beginnings of a beard on his chin.

"I needed to be clean," Lidda said with great dignity, pouring the used bathwater into the bucket in the corner.

Joseph rubbed his nose, hung his thick coat beside Papa's, and only grunted. For that, Lidda was grateful.

She watched Papa tapping the ashes out of his pipe

against the fireplace, then heard his small sigh of satisfaction as he prodded tobacco into the bowl of the long clay pipe. Bending over, so that she could see the round bald spot on top of his head, he picked up a coal in the tongs, held it to the pipe bowl, and sucked vigorously on the stem. In a moment the brown mass glowed red, and a wisp of fragrant smoke curled up to the ceiling.

Everyday life, her family about her: a fire in the fireplace; stew hanging above the flames, bubbling with a rhythmic sound; and Thomas, gnawing on his fist, quiet for once. All of them were together, as if nothing dangerous had ever entered her—as if a foreign, seductive voice had not pierced her mind like a knife stabbing through skin.

3

TITUBA'S HAIR WAS WILD, LIKE SNAKES. Lidda wished she had hair like that, that took off in several directions, seeming to have its own will. Lost in admiration, Lidda stood silently in the shadows of Reverend Parris's kitchen, not wanting to disturb Tituba as her strong dark arms pushed back and forth, forming the elastic bread dough. When she wanted to, Lidda knew how to be quiet, and now her errand was done—bringing a piece of linen to Mistress Parris—she enjoyed watching her friend work, envying the bright red kerchief around her neck.

Tituba smelled different from Mama, who had an odor Lidda hated: sweat, Thomas's spit-up, the midday cooking, chicken feathers, and some herb she used to dose herself with at night because she often suffered from stomach cramps.

Tituba smelled of cinnamon, of lye from washing her master's clothes, of bread baking, and of some indefinable scent that rose from her skin—something like comfort. Was it sweat or something within that came out of the skin? It made Lidda want to jump into Tituba's lap and lay her head against her friend's chest. *Breast. We are not allowed to use that word, "breast,"* Lidda thought, *unless it refers to the breasts of wild beasts in the Bible. If it is in the Bible, it is all right.*

Were there women in the Bible who smelled of cinnamon and baked bread, had wiry hair, and gave off an air of comfort at the same time? Lidda did not think so, unless it was Bathsheba, the woman King David desired. *"Desire." That is another forbidden word, unless we say, "I desire to become a better Christian or a better daughter."*

"I know you back there, Lidda—come out. I see you hiding back there," Tituba said, punching the bread dough down into the bowl. "Come out. It just Tituba."

She turned and grinned, retying the patterned scarf around her hair. Lidda coveted that scarf. The dyed cloth was beautiful and vibrant, especially to Lidda, for red was almost forbidden in their village. There was only one other woman who defied custom, wearing a red waistcoat—Goody Bishop, who ran the tavern outside of town.

Slowly Lidda stepped away from the tall settle. "How did you know I was there?"

"I smelled you. You got a special smell, child, just like I do."

Lidda's mouth dropped. It was as if Tituba had been reading her thoughts. She stepped forward, wanting to hear more.

"What are you doing?"

"Making bread. Don't ask foolish questions. There a lot of foolish people in Salem Village, but you"—she turned suddenly—"not one of them. I know *that*!"

"How do you . . . know that?" Lidda faltered. Her breath seemed squeezed in her throat, like a piece of old meat that would not go down, no matter how hard she swallowed.

"I watch you. You not one of those silly village girls! You different." She lifted the dough out of the bowl and set it on the table.

Lidda did not mind being called different by Tituba. It did not seem like a flaw or a sin, the way it did when her mama or sister called her different. She watched

Tituba knead the dough with a touch so gentle she yearned for it. Her mama's touch was never gentle or light; her fingers poked and prodded, commanding one to be up and about, doing, accomplishing, sweeping, gardening, cleaning. . . . The list was endless. But never just touch for the sake of touching someone else's skin. She longed for that, for a warmth that was sweet as the air in May when apple trees bloomed, the fragrance rising from them like a cloud.

"Trouble come to this house last night. Did Mistress Parris tell you?" Tituba spoke without turning around.

"No, she did not, though she seemed quieter than usual." Lidda would never dare to criticize an elder with anyone else but Tituba.

"Betty—she had a fit."

"What sort of fit?" Lidda moved closer to the fireplace, which gave off a faint heat.

The West Indian slave turned, her face creased with worry. "She fell down, cried out something bit her—pricked her skin—and crawled under the table. Like a dog."

"A dog?" Lidda breathed. She'd wanted to do that sometimes, disappear under the table and let the words rain down without having to answer.

Then a low chuckle escaped Tituba. "But young girls get into trouble, I know, and it funny to see Reverend staring at his daughter like . . ."

"What?" Lidda pressed nearer.

"Like the Devil got in his house!" She clamped her mouth shut and bent over the bread again, giving short, unnecessary pats to the surface, as if trying to calm herself.

Lidda shivered. She did not like any talk of the Devil, especially not after the visitation from that strange creature in the night. Maybe it was only a sort of waking nightmare, brought on by bad food or loss of sleep? Mama always talked about her stomach and about how it kept her awake at night. But that voice; she could hear again its soft, inviting tone. . . .

Tituba turned and looked straight at Lidda. "If Betty had a fever—that be better."

"I hope she recovers soon." Lidda liked the young girl and often sat beside her at meetinghouse, although sometimes Betty started nervously and wrung her hands. Lidda suspected that being the daughter of Reverend Parris might be very uncomfortable indeed. He was not well liked and argued constantly over his rights to fire-wood and his house.

"Mmm-hmmm, time you be getting back, child." Tituba made a shooing motion with her hands toward the door.

Lidda pulled it open to a wind so fierce and cold that it snatched the words of farewell from her lips. She hurried over the packed snow, mindful that visiting with Tituba had made her late for supper. Mama would not be pleased, as if she ever *were* pleased by anything Lidda did or said.

And that is the point, is it not? She never is pleased with you, while I am—most pleased, Lidda. Definitely most pleased.

Lidda stumbled on the path and almost fell. The voice was back. She must have lost her wits to think that bathing would take it away, that she could somehow *wash* it away!

Him! sounded within.

She began to run, snatching at her elbows, gripping her body tightly to try and stifle the voice. Where was it coming from? And what, what was happening to her?

Then there were no more words, just a sense of a hot,

breathing presence. In a quick rush she thought, *Why are you pleased with me?* But there was no answer, although the idea of being pleasing to someone was sweet as wild honey.

Gasping, Lidda rushed toward the door of her house, eager to see Charity and hear Thomas wailing, desperate to pull ordinary life around her like a cloak for protection against darkness and the unknown. Against the voice like a river and the sense that she no longer belonged to herself.

4

THEY WERE ALL SEATED AT THE TABLE, IN their designated places: Papa, lifting his spoon; Mama, mouth drawn tight; Jacob, staring at the door; and Susannah, ready to snap out a disapproving word. Only Charity looked truly welcoming.

"You are late!" Mama said as Lidda hurried to her place on the bench—always to the left of Jacob and Susannah, because they were older. Besides the baby, Charity was the only one who sat to her left as the younger sister—and her favorite.

"I am sorry, Mama, remember I had to bring that linen to Mistress Parris."

Do not say you are sorry when you are not, girl. You are not meant to lie.

Lidda sucked in a breath, which turned into a choking cough.

"What is wrong with you?" Susannah asked. She reached over and thumped her on the back, so that Lidda bent forward, chin touching the cooked pumpkin on her plate.

"Mmmph!" she gasped, as if to signify all was well. Susannah gave her a critical look, one that clearly said, "Why are you my sister? Why not someone else's?" Finally Lidda managed to stop coughing, taking a deep drink of cider.

Papa set down his spoon and began, "I spoke with Reverend Parris today. There are dark things happening in his house, wife."

Mama looked at him, pushing a wisp of hair beneath her cap. Absently, she rocked Thomas's cradle with one foot. "What sort of things, husband?"

"He told me that Betty had a fit last night."

Lidda would have to pretend that she had not talked with Tituba about it. She was sure that Mama would not want her to be friends with Reverend Parris's slave.

"Yes," Papa continued, "a fit, almost like an attack, he said. Her face contorted; she acted as if someone were sticking pins into her; she babbled nonsense and actually crawled under the table!"

There was a chorus of five spoons clinking against their plates.

Without warning, Lidda felt an ominous cloud settling over her; a sense of dread permeated her bones, her skin, out to her fingertips.

"But surely it is some sickness, something we have not seen before?" Mama said. "We live too near the marshes, husband, I have always said that. The fogs that rise from them are noxious and . . ."

To Lidda, the space over the table suddenly seemed distant and faraway. Papa's words, ". . . true . . . wife . . . what . . . say," came in dim, interrupted bursts.

Lidda had the odd sensation that she was floating outside of her body, off to the left. Heat pooled in her stomach, swarming up her chest and the bone between her breasts, surging up her throat, face, and over her head. At the same time, the air around Charity's head began to glow an unearthly red.

With the heat came a terrifying rage, making her want to smash her plate against the wall, rip off her stays, and sweep everything onto the floor in one glorious, noisy mess.

Lidda sucked in a breath and gripped her hands

tightly, sending a dismayed look at Charity, who looked back, nudging her foot under the table.

"What?" she mouthed.

"Hot!" Lidda framed the word, digging her fingernails into her left hand. Heat seared her cheeks, and she feared Mama might notice and ask if she were ill. Pretending to choke on a bit of bread, she put her hands over her face, sheltering behind them so she would not see the scarlet light rimming Charity's head like a bloody omen.

All those years of training to be a "good girl" and a "godly child" stood her in good stead; she would not throw her plate against the wall, she would not jump up and pull things onto the floor. No.

"Are you all right, Lidda?" Mama finally noticed her distress.

"Yes," Lidda murmured from behind her hands. She dared not come out yet, instead forcing herself to stay seated on the bench. It felt like a prison, like the Salem jail, where people beat their fists against the door, shouting to be let out. If she had to sit one more *second*, she would burst into flames and run screaming from the room.

Calm yourself, girl. Think of trees tossing in an icy wind.

Think of cold things. We do not want anyone to notice.

A breath of cold washed over her, and Lidda had an image of the forest beyond Papa's fields, stilled by snow and frost with only the faintest tinkle of ice as the wind passed through. She stood in that space, breathing deeply. Finally Lidda peered out from behind her hands, giving one last cough. The heat was receding, and Charity's head was now its normal blond, with a white cap scrunched on top.

Where did that voice come from? Her middle or her head? Lidda touched her flaming cheeks, giving up all pretense of eating. Did anyone else hear it but her? It was a sibilant voice, soft as a snake's hiss, but somehow attractive and inviting. It seemed to promise things she passionately wanted to know.

She darted another look at Charity, relieved to see that the red light was completely gone. The flush on her own cheeks faded, like water draining away. She could not catch Charity's eye, for she was looking at Papa as he continued the story of Reverend Parris.

"Reverend told me he does not know what to do. He has never seen anything like it before."

"I do not trust those folk he brought with him

from Barbados, husband," Mama said. "Both are dark-skinned slaves—Tituba and her husband, John Indian. What do we know of them?"

Lidda grasped her hands to keep them from trembling. The smells of the food on the table assaulted her nose, making her want to vomit—pumpkin, bread, and the sour scent of cider. Horrible! If her throat were not choked up, she would have leaped into the conversation to say, "Tituba is a good person, a person to be trusted. There are other servants who have dark skin. . . ." But despite her distress she remembered what Mama was alluding to; they all knew of the border wars with Indian tribes, seventy miles north of Salem. The battles were not going well for the settlers, and many refugees had fled south to settle in Salem and towns nearby, bringing tales of cruelty and of whole towns being massacred. Some claimed that the Wabanakis were in league with the Devil and black as the Devil himself, though Lidda did not believe that.

"What you say is true, wife. I wonder he could bring those slaves with him to Salem, as minister of our town."

"But I like Tituba!" The words popped out of Lidda's mouth before she could take them back.

"Did anyone ask your opinion, child?" Papa asked.

"No, Papa," she whispered, breathing through her mouth so that the food smells would not sicken her.

To her right, Susannah sighed in disapproval. It was clear *she* had no such loyalties to Tituba, the foreign-born slave.

You must be more careful, the voice in her head whispered. Lidda found she did not have to talk out loud to speak to this creature, whoever he was—*whatever* he was. *I will.* The words formed in her mind. *I will try.* But if she were good—whatever the voice called "good"—what would she get in return?

Inside her was a soft, amused breathing and a lingering sound. *Meee . . .*

Before Papa finished the grace that signaled an end to the meal, Lidda had already jumped to her feet, clearing the dishes and carrying them to the side table. She noticed Thomas, his mouth an open circle of dismay. "Yaaa," he wailed hungrily. "Yaaaaa!"

Mama bent over to lift him onto her lap, unbuttoning the front of her dress so she could nurse. Despite how fidgety she was, Lidda felt a quick sympathy for her mother's weariness, her sagging breast. Thomas seemed

34

to be sucking out all of her vitality these days.

Quickly Lidda folded a square of wool around her hand and took the pot off the fire. Pouring steaming water into the basin, she scooped soap from the jar and hurriedly began to wash dishes.

"Slow down, slow down, sister, you'll burn yourself," Jacob said kindly.

Lidda gave him a startled look and willed her hands to move more slowly, to wipe the cloth with a measured movement. But she could not say a word to Jacob, afraid it would come out as a shriek.

With one last look at her as he pulled on his coat, Jacob offered, "I'll see to the cows in the barn, Papa. This cold is cruel."

"Yes, son, you do that." Papa stopped to fill his pipe with tobacco, while Charity rose and dried the dishes, setting them on the shelves of the cupboard Papa had built last year. It was convenient having a father who was a carpenter, who could build them cupboards, tables, and bedsteads.

"What is wrong?" Charity whispered.

"What do you mean?" Lidda scoured a plate and handed it to her sister.

"You, jumping in your seat. Your face was all red."

Lips shut! Even Charity must never know . . . I am for you alone.

"Um—it was a sudden thing, perhaps the beginning of a fever, Charity."

"Oh." She accepted the explanation, chattering about the stocking she was knitting, wondering if it would please Mama, who was often difficult to please.

"Knitting!" Lidda hissed under her breath. "I loathe and detest it, and I loathe and detest those needles. . . ." She put her hands to her throat, willing her voice back inside.

And when Papa gave her a questioning look, she felt like bursting into tears or racing outside into the bitter cold.

"Lidda, Lidda." Mama sighed. "You fight so hard against so much, you make me tired."

The words bunched behind Lidda's lips. *Why? Why are we made to knit lumpy stockings and sit on hard benches instead of running beneath the trees and singing?* Biting hard on her lower lip, Lidda managed to keep her thoughts inside. An icy wind blew on her back when Jacob returned, slapping his arms across his chest. A few snowflakes sparkled in his dark hair, and his cheeks were ruddy with cold.

"It is freezing out there. I gave the cows an extra feeding to take them through the night."

"This is the coldest winter I ever remember," Papa agreed. His pipe smoke curled in white puffs toward the low, dark ceiling.

If she did not get outside soon, if she had to stay in here listening to the same words grinding over and over like some hellish millstone circling round, Lidda knew she would not be able control herself much longer.

"Mama!" She threw down the washcloth and seized her cloak from its peg. "Let me see how the chickens are faring. I want to make sure they are warm enough."

"You may go." Mama took Thomas off one breast and settled him with sharp, poking motions onto her right breast. "Goodness, Lidda, you are restless as a clock pendulum! You will need to be calmer if you wish to find a husband, daughter. Men like women who are calm and settled."

Papa sent his wife a fond glance, silently agreeing with her, and Susannah nodded sagely, as if she had all the knowledge in the world about what men looked for in wives, instead of being only sixteen herself.

But Lidda had already grabbed her cloak and was through the door. Racing across the yard, she burst into the barn, shouting,

"I will *not* be settled. I will *not* be calm! I will *never* marry, and if I choose to be restless, so I shall!" Her feet propelled her round and around the barn, whirling faster and faster until she saw small bursts of light, some violet, others yellow like hot stars. After one last breathless twirl, Lidda sank into a pile of hay. Pulling it around her, she snuggled into its sweet-scented comfort, surprised by the unfamiliar sensation of happiness rising up within; it felt like wings, as if she could fly through the barn door into the night sky. She would sail over the village, to see if there was such a thing as happiness in anyone's house. She would know it when she saw it, for it would be colored orange—a soft light that would rim the house of anyone who was happy. They would not feel oppressed by a wrathful God, by sin and shoulds and must nots. Lidda blew out a long breath, repeating, "I will *so* be restless if I wish!"

I do not admire calm girls, and I do not wish you to marry.

"Why not?" Lidda whispered. "Why not marry?"

Because you belong to me.

"But who ARE you?" Lidda shrieked.

You may call me Lucian, light bringer.

Lidda heaped some hay over her middle, burrowing farther into it. It comforted her and gave her a sense of the everyday world that she knew was far behind.

"How do you bring light . . . Luc . . . ian?"

You will find that out in time, girl. I deal in truth and lies, and to you I give the wit to tell the difference.

"Truth and lies," whispered Lidda. She was seized with a sudden lethargy. It would take too much strength to walk back to the house; she would stay here for just a little while until she felt better.

The silence within settled like a midnight river so deep no one could see any movement at all; only at the very edges, near the banks, could a watcher see the ripples of water. Lidda's eyelids closed, and for a few moments, she slept.

5

IN THE GRAY COLD OF THE FOLLOWING DAY,
Lidda slipped out the door when no one was looking
and crossed the snowy field in back. She looked over her
shoulder. They would be calling for her soon. She knew
the faint threads of their voices—each had its own color:
Mama's was yellow, Susannah's was a muddy brown,
and Charity's was pale orange. There were things to
be done—floors swept, ashes carried out, bread dough
kneaded, and Thomas to have his wet clouts changed.

Lidda dragged her boots over the snow, the tops filling with shards of ice. She could not move swiftly today
but instead walked slow as old Goody Osborne. Before
anyone noticed she was not in the privy or the house, she
must get out of sight.

Lidda paused to hide behind a thick hemlock, a
field's distance from the house. It was far too cold for

anyone to come looking for her, she was sure.

Do not be too certain of that.

Lidda slapped at her arms beneath the cloak. Could she *hit* him away? Run so fast that she outran him, leaving him like a wisp of smoke behind?

She tried to leap forward but only managed a slight stagger. It was as if she were swimming through mud, hardly able to move. And her thoughts were slow and cold as the icy field; even her breath was still and heavy in her chest.

She wanted to feel the way she had yesterday in the barn, as if her limbs were full of hot blood, ready to carry her headlong. As if happiness were married to her blood. With that feeling she could outrun anyone, accomplish anything. She remembered the heat pumping through her legs, flowing out to the tips of her fingers as she whirled around the barn. For one glorious moment, she was transformed by color into a creature tinted red by the blood just under her skin, her blond hair streaming back in the darkness. *Like a running sunset*, she thought. But today? Slow and gray, with a leaden weight in her chest that felt like a box filled with grief and remorse. It did not matter anyway; whatever happened, she could not outrun this . . . Lucian.

It is foolish to try, girl.

Lidda pressed her mittened hands to her cheeks, forcing them up so that the world came in as a slit of sky, trees, and snow. With a sob, she let her hands go, then swallowed the next cry. He would not like weakness, of that she was sure. The voice inside was mocking, cutting, as if he was just waiting for her to come to her senses.

How can I come to my senses? Lidda wondered. *I've lost them—how can I get them back? Is there anyone in this village who could help me?*

Lidda pounded her thigh with one hand as she asked each question until her muscles throbbed. But she was no closer to the answer.

Looking about, Lidda realized she was near the frozen stream in Papa's forest, which led deeper into dense thickets she did not want to explore. The tangled woods looked threatening and unsafe, but there *was* no safe place for her now, she knew.

You never cared about safety before, Lidda.

The sun fell on a patch of snow ahead, on the rounded bank of the stream. Kneeling, Lidda leaned forward and swept the snow from the surface. It was not the cloudy white ice that had frozen slowly, thawed, and then refrozen. This was the hard, clear black of a sudden freeze that had grabbed leaves from the stream, fragments of moss, and kept them immobile in its grip.

She leaned closer, eager to see the outline of her face in the ice. There was the curve of her cheek, her frantic, mussed hair, and two smudged eyes. It was not the face of an everyday kind of girl, one who would marry someone from the village or please Mama with her work and neat habits.

The ice blurred. Sudden drops fell, obliterating her faint outline, and though she scrubbed at the ice with one mittened fist, the drops fell faster and faster. For one brief moment, Lidda saw a face that did not look like her own, with two black holes for eyes and two lines running down its cheeks, dripping onto the ice. Something else—some*one* else—was looking out of her eyes.

Gasping, she leaped up and stumbled toward the edge of the woods. There was no one to help her. She was like one of those sailors that Papa talked of, who set out in their ships for a faraway land with only the frailest of instruments to guide them. She had no instrument, no guidance, nothing.

Only me, girl.

She did not answer. It would just make him stronger, and today—in the gray half-light, her boots dragging over the snow—she did not want to talk with him. She wanted to pretend that he did not exist.

6

THEY WERE ASSEMBLED BY THE DOOR, READY
to leave for church in the meetinghouse. The air was
stiff as a set of stays. Lidda held tight to her middle, willing it to be silent and obedient. As if anything about her
had ever *been* obedient! But just for this day, just for this
hour—though truth be told, it would be several hours
by the time services were done—she would behave in a
way that did not make dear Charity's face crinkle with
worry, that did not bring reproaches from Susannah or
weary looks from her mother, who clearly wished for a
different kind of daughter. *Like the other girls in town.*
Not like this girl—me.

She tapped one booted foot against the floorboards,
finally bursting out with, "Susannah! Are you done yet?
What else can you do with your hair?"

Jacob agreed with her. "You are ready, sister, let's go."

And get this agony over with! came the derisive inner voice.

Lidda snickered, then tried to stuff the sound back inside as Susannah brushed past her. "I trust you are not laughing at *me,* sister. I, at least, know how to behave in services. I do what is expected of me." Her lips pulled tight around her teeth, making that familiar, annoying sound, like an old woman clucking to her hens.

Lidda laughed again; she could not help it. Her spirits seemed to rise and bubble inside like hot air, making her laugh. With a quick sideways look, Papa took her arm firmly, steering her through the door. "Your levity is unbecoming, daughter. It is time for sober and serious behavior."

I do not think I know what it is to be sober or serious, Lidda thought. Sober was the opposite of some of the farmers who drank too much hard cider at Goody Bishop's tavern. She had even heard that Goody had introduced a new game called shuffleboard, which sounded like fun. When men played their games at Goody Bishop's tavern and drank too much hard cider, she knew they were not sober as they rolled home. Even though the Bible chastised people for drunkenness, some in Salem had never taken that to heart.

"Papa, did not Noah himself become drunk?" she said gaily, stepping beside her father. Her feet seemed to fly over the ground.

"What is that you say, daughter, about Noah? Are you talking about the Bible? This is the kind of behavior I like to see in you!"

You can thank me that he completely misheard you! Forget about Noah and his drunkenness. Only I know what you search for in the Bible. . . .

No one had yet noticed that on quiet days when she was not needed in the kitchen or the house, Lidda sometimes stole into the other downstairs room where Papa and Mama slept and where Papa kept records of his business. On a table below the small window lay Papa's brown, leather-covered Bible. She would pore through it, looking for tales that described people gone astray, being too angry, perhaps even shoving a lance through an unsuspecting person. She thrilled to the story of Jael, who killed an enemy when she "smote the nail in his temples." "Smote" was a wonderful word. Then there was Tamar, accused of being a harlot by her father-in-law, who was *himself* guilty of immoral behavior.

"Harlot"—she rolled the word over and over. It felt round and solid and carried its own color—definitely red, though she expected there were other words that were yellow or blue or purple.

One day she read of Bathsheba and King David, how he had sent Bathsheba's lawful husband off to the worst of battles, hoping he would be killed so that he, King David, could have the beautiful woman for himself. King David had spied Bathsheba from his rooftop and must have been smitten right away—"smitten" was a wonderful word, of a purple hue. Lidda wondered if she would ever be smitten by anyone in this unlovely town. She thought of the boys she knew, some with pimpled faces, others too serious or quiet for her. None pleased her; none had that spark of wildness she had inside.

Perhaps because she had been chewing on her dry lips, no other dangerous words escaped her mouth as Lidda followed Papa into the dark, cold meetinghouse. There were only a few windows in the walls, letting in a pale winter sunlight.

As she took her seat in the women's section, Reverend Parris was taking his place behind the wooden podium, adjusting his arms in the robes, and sending an accusing look around the room.

"Brothers and sisters, we will begin with Psalm One Hundred Nineteen." And he was off, in love with his round, resonant voice, Lidda thought, sending the words out as if they were solid gold to fall into the waiting hands of the congregation. She looked at Betty Parris and her cousin Abigail, sitting beside Mistress Parris nearby. Mistress Parris had a cowed look, as if being the wife of Salem's minister weighed too heavily on her shoulders. Perhaps Betty had had another fit? Lidda watched as the girl kicked her heels back and forth but was stopped when her mother put out a hand and slapped her legs.

"Rightly so," Susannah murmured. "Swinging her legs in church!"

Then the atmosphere in the meetinghouse changed from a solemn meeting to something more hectic and noisier. "I tell you, friends and neighbors"—Reverend Parris shook one finger at them—"the Devil and his minions surround this village, yes, surround it, circling like wolves ready to bite and harry and destroy. We must be vigilant! We must arm ourselves with scripture, prayer, daily readings, and a spirit of righteousness! This is a test of Salem Village!"

What did he mean by "righteousness"? Lidda wondered.

Doing things his way, girl—never kicking up your heels under the apple trees or singing wild songs. Wearing your stays and always obeying your elders.

Lidda clamped one hand to her mouth, pressing back the laughter that threatened to escape. Silently Charity gripped Lidda's right hand and squeezed it tight.

The words of the Reverend rampaged through the room, hitting the shoulders of the villagers, striking their cheeks; Lidda could almost *see* the force of them. "Devil . . . minions . . . evil . . . seduce . . . destroy!"

Even Papa's head snapped back, and he glanced at his wife with a look that seemed part disapproval and part excitement. Something was thrumming in the air. Once Lidda had seen a bull in a neighbor's field when he scented a cow that had been brought in to be bred; he had lifted his head and snuffled the wind, in the same way that the villagers now lifted their heads and breathed in.

The voice snapped within. *You see how he does this,*

Lidda? He is whipping the village into a frenzy—it is what he wants!

Lidda wondered why anyone would want to stir up such a frenzy, but she was beginning to trust Lucian's observations, and she thought he must be right about Reverend Parris.

On the way home, Susannah elbowed Lidda. "I saw you almost laughing in services, Lidda Johnson! You were not paying attention the way a young lady should!"

"I did pay attention, I did," protested Lidda.

"She did," Charity echoed as she kept a tight grip on Lidda's hand. They both knew she was lying, and Lidda loved her for it.

"Well," said Mama in a distracted voice as they reached their door. She pulled her cloak tighter about Thomas as the wind lifted and slammed into them. "Well, I hardly know what to think . . ."

That is just what he wants, madam—people not knowing what to think.

Lidda ran inside, pulled the pot over the fire, and stirred it up with the poker. To make up for the intruding voice, she helped even more than usual, laying the spoons and bowls on the table and filling a pitcher with cider from the cask.

If I just move fast enough and am good enough, no one will notice what is happening, Lidda thought—*except Charity.* Lidda knew she would have to watch her step to keep her beloved sister from finding out about Lucian and his disturbing presence. It might mean she would have to lie to her, and of all the people in her life, Charity was the one she most hated to keep from the truth.

7

⊱◈⊰

"WHAT THINK YOU, CHARITY?" LIDDA ASKED
as they readied themselves for bed. Taking their clothes
off in one swoop, they leaped into bed still wearing their
petticoats, hoping that some of the warmth trapped
beneath would warm the icy sheets.

"About wh-wh-what?" chattered her sister.

"Betty Parris's fits. Remember Papa spoke of them,
and today in the meetinghouse Reverend Parris kept
thundering about the Devil, being attacked and . . ."
Her voice trailed off as Susannah entered the room, one
hand shielding the flickering candle. Lidda welcomed
the light, wishing they could keep the candle burning
through the night to keep out . . . *him.*

"He is telling us we must be on our guard," Susannah
said, carefully taking off her waistcoat and skirt and laying them on top of the clothes chest, not bundled at the

foot of the bed like Lidda's clothes. "For heaven's sake, Lidda, could you not be a little more *neat*? Husbands like tidy wives." She tied the strings of her nightcap firmly under her chin and climbed into bed, pulling the words around her as if only she were the model of a perfect housewife.

"Well, *you* can be thrifty and neat, Susannah," Lidda grumbled, "but there are more exciting things that I would like in *my* life."

Susannah thumped her head down on the pillow. "Why, what is better than marrying, raising a family, and running a good household?"

Oh, so many things, sister! Lidda thought. Dancing, playing shuffleboard, drinking hard cider, running down the road wearing a red waistcoat, leaving this horrible village . . .

Lidda sighed and did not answer, turned on her side, and hoped that she would be able to sleep. Susannah blew out the candle, and darkness blanketed the room with its chill, restless presence. She did not know if she *wanted* Lucian to appear or if she wished him away. For now.

The next morning Lidda was stirring the porridge in the pot when she felt her thoughts begin to race. Gripping her thigh with one hand, she tried to stop them, breathing deeply and singing a droning hymn within. But it did not work—

I wonder where Lucian goes when he is not within . . . perhaps he lives in some glorious, faraway land where the people are beautiful—not like here—and is that why his voice is so sharp and sometimes cruel when he returns, like Papa's saw cutting through wood—if Lucian does visit other lands with perfect people, I wish I could be like them—somebody easy to talk to, like Ann Putnam, I could be like her, with my cap always neat, and the ready words under my tongue, and after being at the meetinghouse I would go out and talk with my friends, just like an ordinary everyday sort of girl, not the kind of girl with a strange voice inside . . . except he said he did not want an ordinary girl. . . .

Afraid that she might open her mouth and the torrent of words would come pouring out the way milk did from a cow's swollen udder, Lidda grabbed her cloak, mumbled, "Need to use the privy," and dashed outside to the freezing outbuilding. She slammed the door and sat on the ledge beside the hole, rocking backward and forward, moaning, "Oh, no, not again, please . . ." But words could not stop the rush of thoughts inside and the accompanying heat. Her hands trembled violently, and she seized them, trying to still the vibration.

Stop resisting me, girl. It only makes things worse. Let me in.

Lidda clenched her shaking hands and bent over until her head touched her knees. Tears streaked out of her eyes.

Something sighed within. Something arose, making a light sketch on the privy wall—that of a ferociously handsome man with long black hair.

For a moment, Lidda raised her head. "Lucian?"

Yes, I am here, girl, with you always. . . .

How seductive he was, how beautiful, just as Reverend Parris spoke of the Devil, except she did not think Lucian was evil. Something else, but not—the Evil One.

The man on the wall nodded regally and began to reply, but then Charity's voice sounded from outside as she knocked on the privy door. "Lidda? Are you all right? Do you need my help?"

The vivid lines on the privy wall disappeared, piece by piece, until only the rough lumber was left.

"I am"—Lidda smoothed her hair back under her

cap and straightened her cloak—"all right, Charity. I will be back soon," she said through gritted teeth.

She heard her sister's heels crunching on the snow; they sounded reluctant, and if steps could sound worried, these were so. But if Charity had not come, if those lines had stayed, then she could have really *seen* what Lucian looked like—not just a voice, not just an amused and mocking presence.

Something had changed, almost without her knowing it; from a presence she wished to keep at bay and ward off in the night, Lucian and his voice were beginning to entrance her. *He* liked her. *He* was pleased by her. And she was beginning to think that he was more of a gift and less of a burden.

8

LIDDA FINALLY OPENED THE DOOR TO the privy and returned to the house, hoping that her thoughts would behave. She made up an excuse for her absence (*I am becoming proficient at this lying business*) and managed to eat a few spoonfuls of porridge, lumps and all. Papa and Jacob talked of going out into the woods to haul timber for next summer's building projects. As a carpenter, Papa was always in need of good solid lumber, and winter was the time to fell it and bring it back for drying inside the barn.

Once the dishes were washed, Lidda asked, "Mama? Do you need me at home this morning or could I visit Betty Parris? I would like to help her, as you know she had that fit."

"Yes, Lidda, you may go. That is a good and neighborly thing to do."

As Lidda took her cloak off the peg, Papa said,

"Daughter, see if Reverend Parris has any firewood stacked by his door. The townspeople are refusing to give him wood—which they owe him—and I fear that his family does not have enough to burn."

"Yes, Papa, I will look when I go."

"It is not right!" Mama burst out. "They should give him enough for winter and stop fighting with him. I do not like the conflict in this village, it feels like a sickness!"

"Indeed, wife, it is like a sickness, and who knows where it will end?" With those ominous words, Papa pulled on his thick coat and followed Jacob outside.

Lidda was trembling with the effort of appearing to be like the rest of her family. The heat that had swarmed over her while she was in the privy had gone, but its effects had not; inside her head, things were tumbling, turning, and racing like rabbits bounding over the snow.

If Betty is having a fit . . . a fit . . . what does that mean? Are her fits like mine? They could be . . . the thoughts could dart into her head like spring swallows, winging their way and tumbling over and under one another the way mine do . . . and with them comes this strange happiness. . . . I feel as if I could fly to the top of the house, or open a window and soar over the snow . . .

and I would not fall, not ever fall. . . .

By digging the nails of her left hand into her palm, Lidda brought her speeding thoughts under her control. Did *he* do that to her? Was it *his* fault? And where had he gone, anyway? Lucian, he'd said his name was—light-bringer. He was here one moment, then he disappeared and did not speak for days, then reappeared to make funny and cruel comments about the villagers.

"Is there someone else you like better?" she whispered, striding along to the Parrises' house. Her feet felt light as birds' wings; the breath came and went in her chest as a song started up inside. The wild happiness that filled her made Lidda forget that Lucian had not answered her questions.

Knocking on the Parrises' door, Lidda eyed the scant woodpile to one side; it did not look as if it would keep the house warm for more than a few days. In a moment, Tituba answered. Her face was not as cheerful today as it had been the last time Lidda visited. And around Tituba's mouth were marks of worry and an opaque wash at the back of her eyes that looked like fear.

Lidda stepped back. "Are you well, Tituba?"

The woman wiped her hands on her apron and

summoned a tight smile. "I all right, but I worry about Betty—she had more of those fits and now Abigail, too."

Lidda wished there was something she could say to erase the worry lines. Tentatively, she reached out one finger to touch the smooth skin, and she saw tears in Tituba's eyes.

"Go." The woman made a shooing motion with her hands. "Go see the girls. Maybe *you* talk sense to them before . . ." She sucked in a breath.

"Before what, Tituba?"

"Before something terrible happens. . . ."

Lidda hugged her tightly about the middle and ran into the other room, where a fire smoldered in the fireplace. Betty sat as close to the fire as she possibly could without actually putting her legs into it.

Hurrying forward, Lidda knelt by her. "Betty, are you well?"

The younger girl looked at her and brightened. "Lidda! You've come to see me. Have they told you about my fits?"

"Yes, Papa told me, and Tituba."

Betty gave her a puzzled look. "They come on all of a sudden—like, like a storm."

"You do not know when they are coming? You cannot *feel* them before they happen?" Lidda peered into the girl's face intently, wondering if Betty had some of the same symptoms that she had—the sweeping heat, the desperate anger, and colored lights rimming nearby objects. Now she knew enough to dart outside or hide herself in the privy, away from the noticing eyes of her sisters or Mama.

Betty shook her head slowly.

"What is it like when a fit comes upon you?" Lidda asked.

Betty began in a dreamy voice. "My hands clench up, something pricks my skin all over, sometimes my arms freeze, then I have to throw myself onto the floor or I will lose my senses!"

Parts of it sounded familiar—feeling desperate to move, thought Lidda.

"And sometimes, Betty, you babble nonsense," Abigail said from the stool on the other side of the fire. Lidda had not seen her there.

"Yes," Betty said happily, "words just fly out of my mouth!"

"And mine! They fly out of mine, too!" Abigail chimed,

pushing her straggly brown hair under her cap. It looked as if she had not brushed it in days.

"But . . . you do not hear words inside, as if someone is speaking there? Do you ever see red light around someone's head nearby? And do you never feel a terrible anger or a wild happiness?"

The two girls stared at her. "No," they said in unison. Betty added, "That has not happened to us yet. But, Lidda, how would you know of such things?"

Lidda jumped to her feet, shaking out her skirts. "Oh . . . nothing, I heard about it from some neighbor. Just gossip, I suppose." She sighed with disappointment; whatever came upon them, it was not the same as what she suffered. What they had came from the *outside*, and what she had came from *inside*.

"I had a fit, too, the other night," Abigail said importantly, "as if someone were pinching me and pricking me with needles!" Her face was flushed and eyes shining.

"You liked it, didn't you?" Lidda twisted her hands in the folds of her cloak.

For a moment, Abigail's eyes widened, and then she shook her head. "Oh, no, no, Lidda, it was a terrible thing, and we do not know what will become of us. My uncle is fasting this very day, and he prayed over us most of this morning."

Prayed—praying—pray. The words sang inside Lidda's head.

"I think that perhaps I am being punished," Betty said haltingly. "I am not always a good girl—perhaps I have sinned in some way. . . . Papa has spent the day in prayer. . . ."

What could Betty possibly do to deserve any punishment? Lidda wondered.

Just then, Mistress Parris crept into the room. She seemed thinner than the last time Lidda had seen her in church, more insubstantial. Lidda heard she had taken to her bed for the last week, but apparently she was making an effort now to be part of the family. The ribbons on her cap were tied so tightly beneath her chin that it looked as if she could hardly breathe.

"I joined Mister Parris in prayer. Prayer is very efficacious, as we all know," Mistress Parris intoned.

For some it is. Not for others, came the amused voice.

Suddenly, within, Lidda saw a picture of Mistress Parris stretched out on the bed in prayer, the strings of her cap bobbing to one side. She clapped one hand to her mouth to stifle a laugh.

"We must all pray," the older woman intoned. "It is the only thing that will save us."

This time there was a long peal of derisive laughter, followed by a snort.

Now laughter was sneaking past the edges of her mouth, trickling out like some intoxicating smoke. Lidda whirled and dashed into the kitchen, hearing the amazed comments of the woman left behind. "What is wrong with that girl? Did I hear her *laughing*?"

You did indeed, madam, and sometimes laughter is the only response to madness.

Tituba gave Lidda a searching look and put out an arm to stop her headlong dash toward the door. "Child, what wrong?"

"Tituba, I just"—Lidda dropped her voice, trying to be discreet—"cannot help chuckling when I think of your mistress praying on the bed." She hiccupped with laughter. "The ribbons on her cap bouncing up and down . . ."

Tituba gave her a horrified look and gripped her arm tightly. "It not funny, child—dreadful things happen here—I afraid. . . . Leave before you make it worse!"

She pushed Lidda toward the door, flinging it open to a stinging wind.

This was, Lidda thought, the most fun that she had had in many a day. She knew she had worried Tituba, but she could not stop chuckling. Skipping over the packed snow, swinging her arms back and forth, Lidda sang a cheerful melody. And best of all was this: Now she had a friend, a companion inside who—even if he *was* sometimes threatening, and even if he *did* leave mysteriously from time to time—liked her just as she was and always came back.

Of course, girl, I always do.

9

"WHY, ANN, WHATEVER ARE YOU DOING here?" Lidda asked, standing in the doorway to their barn. She had just fed the chickens, tossing the golden corn across the barn floor, watching them skitter and push to get to the food.

Ann, slightly younger than Lidda but with an air of excited importance, stood in front of her. "I had to come and see you, Lidda. Remember how we used to go berrying in the summer? We had fun together." She paused, one finger touching her red cheek. Her cloak cast a shadow over her eyes, and Lidda could not read them.

"Yes," Lidda answered, "we liked picking sky berries. But what brings you here, Ann? Is all well at your house?" That was the question to ask these days, because in several dwellings in Salem Village, it was not well at all. The fits that Betty and Abigail had experienced seemed to be spreading like the mud that welled up out of the roads in the spring, clutching at travelers' feet and at the hooves of the horses. . . . Lidda stopped her rushing thoughts by sucking in a breath of cold air.

"It is . . . well." Ann hesitated. "At my house—for now." She pursed her lips as if she had important news to convey. "But, Lidda, I am afraid."

Lidda was puzzled. Why was it that when these girls said they were afraid, they looked anything *but* afraid? Yet she knew what Ann meant—there was nothing guaranteed anymore; not church, not family, not winter, nor summer.

"It is distressing, these fits of Betty's and Abigail's, and no one knows what or who is causing them."

"But that is what I have come to tell you! Reverend Parris brought in Doctor Griggs. He examined Abigail and Betty and pronounced them under the influence of the Evil Hand!" Ann pushed back her hood with a triumphant gesture.

Lidda was silent.

Ann chattered on, as she always had done, not waiting for Lidda to respond. "He said there could be no other explanation for their fits, for feeling pricked with pins and needles, then rolling on the floor. Sometimes, Lidda"—Ann's voice dropped and throbbed with importance—"I wonder if I might be suffering from them myself."

Lidda reached out to grab her. "How do you know?"

Ann took back her arm with dignity and said, "A dizziness, a tingling in the chest, then cold." She thumped her body. "And sometimes"— she lowered her voice to a whisper—"I feel as if someone were pinching me all over. But how could that be, for wherever I look, the air is invisible?"

The air IS invisible, you foolish girl. Lucian snorted.

Lidda started and almost burst out laughing. Ann's cluster of words reminded her of the chickens pecking at the corn in the barn, bumping against one another and hurrying with outstretched necks to get the food— mindless and full of their own importance.

And now it seemed that Lucian voiced the very thoughts that were in her head. What would he have to say about Ann?

Dangerous. Her family is powerful and land hungry. Do not tangle with her, girl.

Ann gave her a quizzical look and asked, "Are you

not going to invite me inside? It is some time since I have held Thomas on my lap."

"Of course," Lidda mumbled, leading the way to the house. It seemed her manners had deserted her; she had forgotten how to be with friends, how to chatter, how to be easy with them. The girls she once knew had gone on to talk of dresses, marriage, and families, and she had gone in a different direction, climbing trees and attempting to fly with the birds, bearing the sudden heat that blazed over her head. She no longer understood them, and she knew she could never be like them.

Who would want to be like them?

Lidda stumbled on the path, turning her head away from Ann's sharp gaze. She couldn't help brushing one ear with her hand, not sure if she wanted to fix those words more firmly in her mind or to brush them away.

Inside the house, Ann took off her cloak and shook out her skirts, greeting Susannah, Charity, and Mama with grace.

"Where are your brother and Papa, Lidda?" Ann asked, looking about the room.

"Out in the woods, collecting timber," she answered. She suspected that Ann had an eye for her older brother,

Jacob, handsome as he was with his ruddy cheeks and new beard.

Ann held out her arms to Thomas, who was sitting on Charity's lap. "Ah, my little man, there you are!" Ann lifted him up to her shoulder, patting his back and pressing her nose into his neck. He snuggled into her shoulder so that all Lidda could see were his bright dark eyes peering out.

Sometimes Lidda thought her little brother was wiser than his years; his intent gaze followed them around the room, as if he knew what they were thinking. Could he sense the danger sweeping across the village? she wondered.

There was no answer from her baby brother, just his sharp cry of delight as Ann offered him her knuckle to chew on. "Oof! His teeth are sharp. He is getting a lot, is he not?"

Mama patted the front of her dress with a tender motion. "Yes, he is, and yes, his teeth are sharp," but her words did not match the proud look she sent toward her youngest.

Lidda felt a moment's sympathy for her mother and the trials of nursing. It was something to be endured on top of all the other work Mama had to do each day.

"You have heard the news, Mistress Johnson?" Ann looked enquiringly at Lidda's mother.

"About what, child?"

"Doctor Griggs! He examined Betty and Abigail last night and said they were both under the influence of 'the Evil Hand.'"

Susannah shrieked, hands flying to her face. "The Devil, he means the Devil, I know it, just as Reverend Parris has been warning us. The Devil is in Salem Village!"

Lidda met Charity's eyes and thought that her sister knew just how much Susannah was enjoying this moment.

"That is a serious accusation Doctor Griggs has made, Ann," Mama said, taking Thomas back onto her lap.

Ann took up her cloak, swirled it around her, and prepared to leave. It seemed she, too, enjoyed the dramatic moment. "He said there was no other explanation for the strange postures, the chills, and the feeling of being pinched and stuck with needles. What else could it be?" She looked around the room and, making an excuse that her mother needed her at home, sped out the door.

A silence followed her, the kind of silence Lidda heard after a great storm had thundered over the house, shaking the roof tiles and lashing the trees outside. It was as if all of them were taking a deep breath at the same time.

Evil Hand! She knows nothing of this.

Lidda pressed her fingers to her chest, to the place where she thought the voice came from. How did he know? What did he know of evil anyway? What if—what if he was part of this, causing the heat that sailed up her body and her wild whirling thoughts?

Stop your questions, girl, and do not share them with anyone.

"But why not?" she whispered, earning a stare from both Charity and Susannah.

Because I have other plans for you. And if . . . you . . . tell, I will abandon you to your fate. To emphasize his words, Lidda felt a shock to her whole body, something that lanced all the way down to her toes.

Rocking backward, she whispered, "All right."

"What is all right, Lidda?" Susannah said angrily. "I swear you become odder and odder with each passing day. How can it be *all right* to have the Devil loose in

Salem Village? How *can* it be?" She thrust out her hands and waved them.

No one answered her; there was nothing to say, and when Jacob and Papa burst through the door bringing the same news of Doctor Griggs with them, they found the rest of the family strangely silent, almost unwilling to talk about the doctor, the two girls, and the dire pronouncement.

But Lidda knew, with a clarity that was like a candle in a dark room, that all had changed. Something was loosed in the village, Devil or not, and they would pay for it, every last man, woman, and child—every horse— every stalk of corn—each lopsided building left to molder in the ruined fields. She saw it all inside, brown and pitiless, the color of hatred.

And do not forget the dogs.

10

LIKE A MOTH DRAWN BACK TO A CANDLE flame, Lidda found she could not stay away from Betty Parris's house, as if there—tucked among the jumbled furniture, the plates, the scant firewood stacked by the door—she would find the answer to the questions that tortured her.

Is Lucian evil or good?

What does he want? Why me?

What will I do if someone discovers him? Would I be accused of being under the Evil Hand, too?

Twisting her hands together as she'd seen Betty do at church, Lidda told Mama that she needed to visit Betty again and ran off through the sharp, unsettling snow. She did not look up at the pale sun, or see the white smoke puffing out from the chimneys; all she saw were her feet stepping one in front of another. "I am going to see Betty and Abigail, I am going to see Betty and Abigail. . . ." If she repeated that often enough, she would reach her destination and not get lost in her murky thoughts.

Once inside the house, she noticed Tituba bent over a mixing bowl, stirring something slowly, two stirs to the right, two to the left, then another one to the right. The woman was so intent on what she was doing that she did not hear the sound of the door closing.

She started when Lidda asked, "Tituba! What are you making? Something for Reverend Parris? I heard he met with some other ministers about Betty and Abigail."

"Yes, girl, he did." Tituba looked up, darting a sideways glance at her husband, John, who leaned against the table, watching the mixing bowl as if it might contain the very answers Lidda was searching for.

"They say be patient. That what they say." Tituba gave an extra-hard stir with the wooden spoon.

"Hello, John Indian," Lidda said, suddenly shy. He was a quiet, swarthy man with dark eyes, a compact body, and a sense of being complete within himself. He nodded in her direction.

Tituba said hastily, "Go see the girls—visit with them."

"I will," Lidda answered.

Tituba nodded and went back to the mixing bowl, teeth gripping her lower lip in concentration.

When Lidda went into the other room, she found the two girls sitting as close to the fireplace as they could without actually catching fire. Mistress Parris was nowhere to be seen, nor was the Reverend.

Wrapped in a thick shawl, Betty looked up, her pinched face alight with interest and something else Lidda could not name—something that looked like shyness and excitement mixed together.

"Lidda! I am glad you are here. So much is happening!"

"Important things," her cousin Abigail chimed in.

Crouching beside the younger girl, Lidda held her stiff hands out to the fire, hoping to find a touch of warmth. She did not dare take off her cloak, for it was almost as cold inside the house as outside.

"Lid"—Betty lowered her voice—"you shall never believe what is happening. It is most exciting, and I vow that it has never been done before—at least in Salem Village, it has not."

"Has not," Abigail echoed.

"Then tell me," Lidda said impatiently.

"Tituba is making a witch cake!" Betty's tone was triumphant.

"A *what* cake?" Lidda thought she had not heard correctly. Perhaps it was a sort of grain that she had no knowledge of, something that Reverend Parris had brought from his days in Barbados, something like switch grain or twitch grain. Her mind played with the words, imagining how the grain would grow . . . in great leaps and bounds under the hot Barbados sun . . . fantastic green leaves twining up supports, reaching for the sky . . . the vines would grow darker, larger . . . almost threatening passersby as if the vines might make a grab for their ankles . . .

"A WITCH CAKE!" Betty said loudly and deliberately. "To find out who is putting these dreadful spells on Abigail and me."

"A witch cake," Lidda repeated dully, reining in her racing thoughts with difficulty. This did not bode well. It felt forbidden, soiled, like a married man running away with a pretty servant girl.

"Mistress Sibley from church told our Tituba and John Indian how to do it." Betty tapped her right foot against the floor, seemingly happy that, at long last, something was being done about her fits.

"Mistress Sibley," Abigail breathed, as if that name made this strange venture respectable. "But we mustn't tell Reverend or Mistress Parris. It is a secret!" Abigail's face glowed.

Lidda could not reconcile her image of Mistress Sibley—a cheerful-faced young matron, respected in the village and a member of the church—telling Tituba to make a witch cake. This did not come from Barbados, where the West Indian slave had lived, but from Salem Village. Why would Tituba agree to something that spoke of witchcraft?

Abigail continued eagerly, "We had to collect our urine from the chamber pot last night and give it to John Indian, who mixed it with rye meal. He will bake it on the coals."

"A cake!" Lidda seemed stuck in nonsensically repeating everything the girls said. Anything less like a cake she could not imagine. "And what will that do?"

"Then Tituba will feed it to the dog to see if he gets the same symptoms that we do—rolling about, freezing, being pricked with pins . . . or the dog could point to the witches who are hurting us. The witch who is causing this harm might even cry out in pain." The girls shared a conspiratorial glance, seizing each other's hands and holding on.

"How will you know?" Lidda said bitterly. "Will it tell you? Will the dog strike its paw against the ground, two times equals an A, three equals a B?"

"Clearly you do not believe this, Lidda Johnson, but something must be done!" Abigail thumped her hand on her lap with each word. "We must stop the oppression by witches in this town."

Abigail's self-righteous, punishing tone was clear—someone would pay for their suffering.

Pushing one hand against the cold floorboards, Lidda rose and went back into the kitchen. Both John and Tituba were crouched before the kitchen fire, watching a round shape bake in an iron spider over the embers. At a nod from his wife, John leaned forward and pushed the pan off the coals. Quickly Tituba bent and lifted the cake onto the table.

"Phew!" John said under his breath. "It stinks, wife."

"Of course it stinks, husband!" Tituba gave him a scornful glance.

Betty and Abigail crowded into the kitchen, pressing

close to Lidda as they gathered around the table. The five of them stared intently at the warm cake, as if willing it to divulge its answers then and there. Perhaps the steam rising from it would spell out a name or, at the very least, the first letter of the name of the witch oppressing these girls, if such a thing were possible.

Lidda leaned closer, inhaling the raw, acrid stench of urine mixed with baked rye, but the steam did not form any letter or name that she could see. She had a sudden, horrid premonition that they would never know the answers, that they would all stay embedded in this mystery like an ox stuck in the mud that could never climb out and eventually died . . . there would be no escape.

She shuddered, clapping one hand to the back of her neck as Tituba gave her a quick glance. "What, child?"

"I fear this," Lidda whispered. "I fear this."

"But something must be done," Betty said importantly.

"Not tell Reverend, ever," Tituba said quickly. "Now, John husband, fetch the dog, and we see. . . ."

John returned, dragging a small matted dog by its rope up to the table. Putting the cake down on the floor, Tituba stood aside, twisting her hands in her apron. All of them stepped back a pace, watching the dog. He lowered his head, sniffed at the cake, drew away, went closer, and sniffed again. It appeared he could not believe what he smelled or had no experience of this scent.

He sat on his haunches and scratched one ear vigorously, nose twitching.

"Come on!" John said, clapping his hands. "Come on, beast!"

The dog sniffed again, then took a tentative bite of the witch cake. He chewed and swallowed, lowered his head again, and devoured it in three enormous bites.

They all clapped and cheered as Betty exclaimed, "He did it, he ate the cake, now we shall know who it is!"

They steadied themselves against the edge of the table to watch.

"What think you?" Abigail whispered, staring at the dog. "Will he lead us to the witch that oppresses us? How will we know?"

"I not know, child, just Mistress Sibley told me—do this, so I done it."

The dog scratched one ear again, lay down, sniffed his behind thoroughly, licked one paw, then curled up by the fire to sleep, apparently well satisfied with his meal and the rare treat of being close to a fire once again.

"I had hoped," Betty started.

"We thought . . . ," Abigail said, tugging on her mussed hair.

John ventured, "Mistress said . . ."

What a waste of good rye meal. Foolish humans.

Lidda turned and fled out the door, frantic to leave the atmosphere in that house, the stench of fear, lies, and stupidity that burned the back of her throat like bile rising. Even the crisp, cool snow falling on her head could not erase the smell of the cake or the image of them ranged about the table, waiting for a truth that never came.

11

A STRONG GUST OF WIND RATTLED THE panes in the window, waking Lidda. The bedclothes were tangled about her, and sweat ran down her face. That same dream again—of a tall tree on a rocky hill with bodies hanging from the branches, swaying in a hot wind. And she, watching, unable to do anything to prevent what was to come. She lay in the dark, pressing closer to Susannah for comfort. It was as if at night a truce was declared, and they could sleep side by side with none of Susannah's complaints about Lidda's dreaminess and how different she was from the other village girls.

Lidda turned and settled on her right side, drawing the covers tightly over her ears. Sleep had become an enemy instead of a place of refuge, a place where even though Lucian was silent, his presence shaped her dreams and nightmares. Some of the scenes beckoned to her, promising delights—white cliffs overlooking a deep blue sea, which crashed and foamed on a stretch of sand; long stretches of hilly land with upright stones on them that spoke in echoing voices. Other times, her dreams were surrounded by a black, noxious fog that she could not break through. Then she would wake gasping, sweating, wondering what was to become of her.

Lidda stared into the unfriendly dark, thinking about her visit to Reverend Parris's house some days ago. She could not erase from her mind the image of that mangy dog gulping down the witch cake, and how they had waited for him to point his nose at a witch or do *something* to help them solve this dire mystery.

But nothing had happened except that the miasma of fear had thickened about Betty and Abigail, Reverend Parris, and his wife. When Reverend Parris found out about the witch cake, he was livid and delivered a thundering rebuke in church to Mistress Sibley, who burst into tears, wailing that she had made a mistake. But through it all, Lidda remembered the avid faces of the girls in church who suffered these fits—whatever the cause. Now this plague was spreading to other girls in the village—young Ann Putnam and Elizabeth Hubbard. They, too, claimed to be bitten and pinched and would fall down as if their bones had turned to ice, freezing them in strange, unnatural postures.

What was it Betty and Abigail had said several times? Betty told Lidda that she had to roll under the table or she would lose her senses.

Even I used those words that night when I feared I would burst into flames if I did not escape outside to the barn. But what did it mean to lose one's senses? There was Goody Good, who did not appear to have all her wits about her. She wore ancient, worn clothes, smelled strongly of cow dung, and wandered from house to house begging, dragging her children with her. One man had even let her sleep in his barn for a while before casting her out, afraid she might set his building on fire.

People feared Goody Good. After having a bit of bread pressed into her hand, she would mutter incomprehensibly and stump off again. Mama once said, "I never know if she is cursing me or blessing me."

So if she, Lidda, lost her senses, would she dress in horrid, ancient clothes that smelled of manure and traipse about the village, muttering and frightening people?

I will not let that happen to you, girl. I promise. I have better things in mind for you.

And what good is the promise of a . . . She faltered. *Whatever or whoever you are? Spirit or a dream?* Lidda fired back in her thoughts.

I always keep my promises, girl; you should know that. I promised to be your companion, and so I will be.

But you do not always feel like a companion, Lucian, though sometimes you make me laugh, and you are company—of a sort.

Of a sort! The voice was offended.

You frighten me sometimes, and you are there in the heat over my head when I have to rush out to the privy, hide my face, and lie to my sister Charity, dearest of all in the whole world to me. . . .

Dearer than me?

She paused for a second, brought Charity's face to mind, and whispered, "Yes, dearer than you!"

There was an answering silence that thrummed with hidden energy, stretching out, broken only by the window rattling in the storm and by Susannah breathing loudly into her ear.

Do you want to see me, Lidda? Really see me? This time

87

the words were warm, inviting.

Yes, I do, she thought, pressing the edge of the blanket to her mouth.

Then, like something becoming clear under the surface of a rushing stream, piece by piece the creature assembled himself so that Lidda could see him inside the darkness of her head: He unfolded his body, starting with his long, elegant feet; up his lean legs, encased in shining black breeches; his bare torso became visible, gleaming as if from distant firelight; then his long, smooth arms and hands with exquisite pointed fingers; and last his head, which was frighteningly handsome, more glorious than anything she had ever known, with black hair cascading down his back, waving in an invisible breeze. Complete, there, unlike anything ever seen before in the drab confines of her village.

But his eyes! Silver like a running stream—a straight nose—and a mouth that curved in an intimate smile over pointed teeth.

Lucian, she called silently. *That is your name.*

Yes, I bring light to this mad village to show you the lies of those witch girls.

There was a sudden, raucous laugh inside—like

nothing from this world. If it erupted in church, all the straitlaced men and women would jump up and race about, flailing their arms and perhaps hurling curses. If someone heard it outside, he would gallop over the frozen fields, bareheaded and bare chested, into the dark, unfathomable woods beyond. Woods that were as impossible to know and full of danger as Lucian himself. But was he truly a danger?

Do not forget delights, girl. I am full of delights. I will show them to you, and you will have a life, a real one—not a pinched, squeezed-in excuse for a life. I will always be here to talk to—unlike your other "friends."

And I, too, will have—

His voice was cut off as Susannah turned over, murmured suddenly, and threw an arm across Lidda. Lucian vanished, and she was left with empty hands and a head that echoed, mourning something she did not know she needed, and wishing to kick Susannah into perdition for interrupting the sight of the most beautiful creature she had ever seen. Her friend. Hers.

12

LIDDA TESTED HER FEET ON THE FLOOR THE next morning. Would she be the same? Could she walk as usual after seeing—*him?*

"Whatever are you doing?" Susannah snapped, slipping into her cold shoes. She shivered, complaining. "I cannot wait for spring. I am so tired of freezing beds, stiff shoes, icy petticoats. . . ." She pulled on her moss green skirt, fastening it at the waist, then straightened her linen cap on her head. Even Susannah seemed affected by Lucian's visit last night, Lidda thought; she seemed frazzled, nervous, not quite herself.

Lidda did not answer as Susannah left the room, heading downstairs where the sounds of Thomas's wails rose clearly.

Hurriedly, Lidda dressed, shuddering and thumping her arms across her middle. *Are you there?* she asked, but there was no answer. Where did he go when he was not inside?

Tucking her flyaway hair under her cap, Lidda ran downstairs to find Charity walking Thomas about the room, trying to sing over his crying. He did not want to be comforted; his wails bounced off the ceiling beams, piercing the ears of all present.

"What a set of lungs that boy has!" Papa declared. "I shall go out to the barn and see how the stock are faring." He rose suddenly from the table, leaving his empty plate and mug.

"I shall come with you," Jacob announced, rising as quickly as Papa had.

"Men!" Susannah said from her place on the bench. "A little wailing sends them running. . . ." Her words were drowned in the sound of the rising cries.

"Hush," Mama said loudly, holding out her arms for Thomas. But he would not be calmed; his howling reached a crescendo as his face purpled and eyes squeezed shut.

"Let me take him," Lidda mouthed. She carried him over to the fire. "See the pretty flames, Thomas?" she crooned, bending from side to side. "See how they are orange and red and yellow. . . ."

She began to dance, twirling in place and swaying back and forth. As she moved, Thomas's cries faltered; he sniffled and hiccupped, then he subsided.

"Lidda! Dancing is forbidden!" Susannah jumped up to stop her.

"Not when it calms a colicky child!" Mama retorted. She sent a grateful look toward Lidda, who dipped and swayed and twirled, happy to be allowed to move about. Thomas laughed and chortled, then suddenly his eyes closed, and he fell silent.

"There, little one, there." Lidda tucked him beneath his blanket in the cradle. "Sleep—and keep warm."

The wind gusted outside, scouring the clapboards as if the house itself were some huge cradle that it would rock violently from side to side. With a thump of the door, Papa and Jacob returned, bearing armloads of wood and depositing them near the fire. They settled on the bench, holding out their hands to the flames.

"I wonder what is happening in town today," Susannah said, mending a petticoat. She looked up as Lidda stared at her; there seemed to be altogether too much *pleasure* in her sister's tone, as if she delighted in the chaos of the village.

"Well, I *do* wonder, sister, don't yo[u]
is spreading to other girls in the village?
with Ann Putnam, are you not? Now she is
well, and Elizabeth Hubbard, and . . ." She wa[ved]
needle, and the firelight caught on it so it flamed
"Soon there will be others, I am sure."

"Yes, it is disturbing, Susannah." Papa took up a
piece of wood to whittle. "It is like a wind blowing over
the village, and who knows which house it will buffet
next?" He rubbed his eyes and looked perplexed by the
events that he had no explanation for, that did not fit
into any of his neat categories of home, church, family,
God, beasts, crops, firewood, and carpentry.

Suddenly, from outside came the sound of tramping
feet and voices. Lidda ran to the door and opened it a
crack to peer through.

Three men, stout in their winter garments, walked
past, talking together. One of them had a piece of parch-
ment clutched in a gloved hand.

"We will get Tituba first," he said, and Lidda realized
it was Mister Putnam with two friends.

"Then we shall get Goody Good," said another, "and

she is ill in bed."

e men. "She must still

id the third man, who

am's brother, Edward,

his hat. "Finally, Betty

that oppresses her."

d the word "that" and

s were not considered

Of course not, girl. What are you thinking of?

There was a raw edge of anger in his voice that alarmed Lidda, making her open the door wider, despite Susannah's shrieks. She poked her head out to watch the three men turn right onto the small beaten path leading up to Reverend Parris's house and knock loudly on his front door.

His door swung open, and someone peered out, materializing into the Reverend with his long face, disordered clothes, and a thin, righteous mouth. Had he known they were coming?

"LIDDA, SHUT THE—" Susannah screamed, but the words stopped abruptly as Papa hurried forward, looking outside as well. Lidda heard the decisive thump of her sister's shoes as she followed, eager to learn what was happening.

"Fetch Tituba for us, Reverend Parris."

The rest of the family crowded behind Lidda to see the drama being enacted.

After a moment, Tituba appeared, wrapped in her shawl. The door creaked wide, she was handed off to Mister Putnam, and the door slammed shut with a final sound, as if it were glad to see the back of her.

"But, sir, I done no wrong!" Tituba said. "I done nothing! Only the witch cake and that Mistress Sibley's idea!"

Mister Putnam seized the slave's arm firmly, marching her over the trampled snow. "The girls have accused you, Tituba, and the law says that we must take into custody all those accused of being witches."

"But I not a witch!" Tituba wailed, stumbling along beside the men.

Lidda darted out into the freezing wind, intending to run after Tituba to protect and defend her.

"You shall not go!" Papa jerked her back inside and slammed the door. "This is not our business.

Some-one has to answer for the plague that has come upon those poor girls, and who more likely than that foreign-born slave woman?"

"And Goody Good, I wager," Jacob said. "With her strange ways and odd mutterings, she looks like a witch!"

"Hush," Lidda surprised herself by saying. "Hush! We know nothing about this, nothing at all! We do not even know if there *are* such things as witches!" The words escaped her mouth before she could bring them back.

Tsk. That was not wise, girl.

"Daughter!" Mama lifted her hands. "Of course there are witches. Do not let anyone in the village hear you saying that! It is in the Bible—'thou shalt not suffer a witch to live.' Remember that family in Boston some years back—"

Papa broke in, continuing the story. "The children had the same symptoms as these girls in our village— falling on the floor, claiming to be pinched and pricked with pins—all the same. It was the Irish washerwoman who oppressed them."

Lidda set her lips together in a mutinous line; they did not know what they were talking about. The girls did not know what they were talking about either. She was not sure *how* she knew, she just did—down in the core of her body. She remembered the gleeful tone Abigail had used in describing her fits, and how Betty's eyes had sparkled when she told of being pricked and pinched. It was not witches.

Lucian had said that the girls lied. But then, what was the explanation for all of this?

A cloud settled on her chest—a dark and strange sensation. The rest of her family clustered around the fire, talking about the day's wondrous events; what would happen next? Would there be an examination of the women to find out if they were, in fact, witches?

Lidda could not think of an examination or what the future held. All she saw was her friend being hustled down the street, arm bent at a cruel angle by Mister Putnam, her anguished voice crying out, "But I done nothing wrong. Nothing!"

13

PAPA STOOD BY THE DOORWAY, BUNDLED in his outdoor clothes, with Mama beside him in her thick russet cloak. Thomas was tucked securely within its warm folds, asleep for once. The rest of the family stood ranged behind them, waiting.

"The magistrates first met at Ingersoll's tavern," Papa said, smoothing his graying whiskers. "But it was too crowded, too many people wanting to see those women questioned about this dreadful plague."

"Dreadful plague," Susannah intoned, like a refrain to one of the doleful hymns they sang in church.

"What think you will happen to your friend Tituba?" Charity plucked at Lidda's cloak.

"I know not," Lidda whispered back, "but I fear this town. When people are afraid, they can be cruel." *How do I know* that? she wondered.

Papa marched outside, leading them down to the

meetinghouse. A crowd was already gathered in front of the door, waiting for it to open.

Suddenly it swung wide, and the villagers pushed and crowded their way into the cold building, wearing their warmest clothes and cloaks. They knew that the meetinghouse would be even chillier than the outside, for though it was March first, the sun shed no warmth on the scene below.

Lidda slipped inside, holding Charity's hand, following Mama and Susannah to the women's side, while Papa and Jacob went over to the men's section. Their boots rang on the wooden floor. Lidda noticed that the girls—Betty, Abigail, and Ann Putnam—sat together at the front of the room.

Mama pulled Charity and Lidda down onto the hard bench. "Quickly, girls, you can see they are about to begin."

At the head of the large room was a big table, and beside it stood a man who introduced himself as John Hathorne, along with "the other magistrate, Mister Jonathan Corwin. We are in charge of the proceedings here this day, and we shall be interrogating these three women."

"Poor Goody Osborne," whispered Charity. "I heard

she was ill in bed when they fetched her."

"Hush!" Mama said.

Mister Hathorne called in an important voice, "Bring in Goody Good for questioning."

The woman stumbled on the way to the table, where she stood before the magistrates. She looked worn, confused, and none too clean. Her clothes were obviously someone's castoffs, with patches and ill-made darns in the skirt, and a shawl around her shoulders that would have done better duty as something to warm baby pigs in the barn. It was hard to believe that she could be the mother of a young daughter.

"Sarah Good," John Hathorne began, "what evil spirit have you familiarity with?"

"None," she mumbled.

"Have you made no contract with the Devil?"

She turned her head to one side. "No."

"Why do you hurt these children?"

She peered around with a grumpy, surprised expression. "I do not hurt them, I scorn it!"

Lidda trembled as the questions fell on the woman's shoulders like hammer blows, with the examiner asking why Good went away muttering from the Reverend's house. Good replied that she was thanking him for helping her child.

"Have you made no contract with the Devil?" the magistrate repeated loudly.

"No."

Then he asked the afflicted girls to look upon Sarah Good and see if she was the one who hurt them.

Immediately, they fell into frozen postures on the floor, arms stuck out, legs askew, with their faces drawn into agonized expressions. The crowd talked excitedly among themselves.

"How do they *do* that," Charity whispered, "all together at the same time?"

"Lies!" Lidda whispered back. Hadn't she just seen Ann twitch her skirt before they all fell to the floor? It looked like a signal to her.

Then Sarah Good was led away and Goody Osborne was helped up to the table, with faltering steps. *She looks too feeble to hurt a mouse!* Lidda thought.

Exactly! Lucian responded. *They prey on the weak, who are easy targets.*

Lidda had trouble paying attention to the questions demanded of Goody Osborne, just like those asked of

Sarah Good before: Why did she hurt the children? Had she made a contract with the Devil?

Hands clenched, Lidda waited for them to bring out her friend. Finally, Goody Osborne was helped into a seat where she collapsed, pale and sick looking, the thin linen cap on her head looking as tattered as she must feel.

Jonathan Corwin led Tituba forward, holding her arm firmly as if to prevent her flying away. That tight grip, more than anything, told Lidda that the conclusion to this examination was already foregone. They assumed her friend was guilty, a witch, capable of harming children, and must be held down: Tituba, who smelled of baking bread, whose apron was always warm and clean, who talked to Lidda in a kind voice that made her think of coconut palms—Tituba had told her once about them—the white sand beaches with a turquoise sea lapping softly, where children played naked in the water—what would it be like to be naked in turquoise water? Lidda thought she would die from bliss if she ever found herself without clothes, surrounded by warm, buoyant, salty water filled with brightly colored fish—

You would like being naked, girl. No stays or petticoats

to trap you like a snared rabbit.

Lidda shivered, trying to keep her eyes on what was in front of her instead of seeing the heavenly images inside. Gripping her hands together, Lidda watched the magistrate call the room to attention. The entire assembly stopped talking, eyes fixed on the accused woman.

The man's voice rang out. "Why do you hurt these poor children? What harm have they done to you?"

The slave woman shook her head. Her kerchief was askew, and she looked as though she had not slept in days. This morning Lidda had heard Jacob telling Papa that the accused women were being held in the village jail, a place of tiny cold cells without enough room to stand up in. What cruelty!

You are surprised by that?

No, she said silently, *I am not*.

Then Tituba answered the magistrate's question. "They do no harm to me, I no hurt them at all."

"Why have you done it?"

"I done nothing. I cannot tell when the Devil works." Her voice wavered.

"What does the Devil tell you to do?"

"He tells me nothing."

103

The room rustled, and there were a few low cries at her admission, "He tells me nothing." Tituba was *admitting* to being in league with the Devil; Lidda's stomach felt hard and cold as a stone. What had they done to her friend?

"Do you never see something appearing in some shape?"

Charity pressed closer to Lidda, who was shaking, despite her clenched fists and warm cloak.

"Tell the truth, who it is that hurts them!" the magistrate said loudly.

"The Devil for anything I know!" Tituba held up her head for a moment, her eyes flashing.

Lidda thought she saw marks on the side of her friend's cheek, swollen and bruised looking; she suspected that Reverend Parris had beaten her to make her confess. It would be like him to do so—to preach God out of one side of his mouth and then hit his slave woman.

You see who is the cruel person in this room, girl!

Lidda nodded in response to Lucian's comment, holding on to the sound of his voice to anchor her in this room full of shifting, whispering people.

The magistrate continued in a penetrating voice.

"What shape does the Devil take when he hurts them?"

"Abigail and Betty?" Charity whispered to her sister, who nodded.

"I saw a thing like a man that told me to serve him— I said I would not—it was Goody Good and Osborne that hurt the children—not Tituba!"

The words came slowly and haltingly, as if she were plucking them out of the air one at a time. They had a desperate feel to them. Lidda could see her looking from one magistrate to the other, trying to read their faces for signs that would help her.

She continued, "They told me hurt the children, but I said, not Tituba, I afraid of God." She looked up at the magistrate—was this what he wanted?

The back of Lidda's throat burned with acid. They were wringing these words out of her friend, forcing her to admit to consorting with the Devil, making her accuse the other two women—poor souls who never harmed anyone except that one muttered and the older one had made the mistake of marrying her Irish servant. Apparently that was an unforgivable offense in this village.

Forgiveness! You jest!

The magistrate continued relentlessly, asking how

105

the Devil appeared to Tituba. She answered again, darting quick glances at him,

"Sometimes like a hog, sometimes like a great black dog—four times."

There was a collective gasp from the onlookers.

"But I said I not serve you."

A look of satisfaction crossed Mister Hathorne's face, almost softening the grim lines that ran from his nose down to his mouth. Lidda stared at them. What made those lines? His hurtful thoughts? His hatred of witches? Hesitantly she raised one hand to her face and traced the skin around her nose, then down to her mouth and chin. Nothing. No lines, though you would think that the shock of walking about with this *creature* within—

Lucian, my name is Lucian. And his sour nature produces those lines on his face.

She jumped, and Charity touched her arm, a worried look on her face. "What is wrong?"

"Stomachache," Lidda whispered. Mister Hathorne's voice took on a hectoring, excited tone.

"Any other animals?"

"A bird."

The crowd talked and jostled together—first a hog,

106

then a big dog, now a bird?

"A small yellow bird," Tituba continued, "and two cats, one red and the other big as a little dog." Her voice gained in speed and confidence as she saw the pleased expressions of the magistrates and heard the excited cries of the audience. She ended in a loud voice, "They said serve him."

"Did they hurt you?" the magistrate asked.

"They did scratch me after I prayed, because I said I not serve them."

"What did they want you to do?"

"Hurt the children."

Lidda closed her eyes. Tituba was lying. She could *smell* the lies—at first they were like soot, like a fire badly put out, then like vomit at the bottom of a bucket— a fierce, sour stench. Suddenly she straightened on the hard bench. Was *this* part of Lucian's influence? It seemed to her that she saw things more clearly, smelled scents she had never noticed before, and had extra senses to detect lies and to see the truth.

The questions went on and on, as Tituba sagged at the knees, only held up by the other magistrate's strong grip. Breathing rapidly through her nose, Charity clutched

Lidda's hand even harder. Lidda could sense fear in her, mixed with the rancid odors rising from the men and women crowded together, their eager faces glistening with sweat, letting out cries of wonder and anger with each new revelation. The noise of the crowd swelled and boomed like approaching thunder.

Lies, all lies.

I know that, Lidda said silently, *but what can I do? I cannot stop this.*

An inner silence answered her as Tituba confessed she had ridden on a pole with Good and Osborne behind; that the two women commanded her to kill Mister Putnam's child, Ann; and that Goody Osborne rode with a creature that was "all over hair, all the face hairy and a long nose and I don't know what it is. I can't name it."

Rising slightly from her seat, Lidda stared at Tituba, willing her to look at her, to see one look of kindness, to see someone who thought no evil of her. For one moment, it seemed the slave woman lifted her bruised face and glanced over at Lidda. Her eyes flickered briefly, then she turned her attention back to the two men questioning her.

Lidda subsided on the bench, her insides boiling

with anger. They had lost their senses, every last one of them, except, perhaps, she, Charity, and Tituba. Her throat ached with repressed words that felt like vomit about to hurl out of her body: "You all lie! These women are not witches!" Lidda grabbed her throat with both hands, pressing the words back inside. If she spoke now, she would be accused just as they had been. If the magistrates learned of Lucian and how he talked to her, would she not be sitting in the examiner's chair destined for hanging?

The only answer to all of her feverish questions was a long indrawn breath, then a sigh that ended in a derisive snort. *Humans!*

14

LIDDA FELT CRUSHED AND EMPTY, LIKE THE
outer leaves of a dry cornstalk blistered in the wind. The
examinations of the "witches" took days, and the entire
village had gone for every session. Each day the women
seemed to grow smaller, to diminish, with the examiners
seeming to swell with the amazing and astonishing hap-
penings. And each day the girls continued to fall on the
floor in fits, crying out, appearing to be in deep agony.

At last it was over. She could breathe again. At supper
Lidda asked, "Where have they taken them, Papa?"

"The witches?" Papa paused, spoon halfway to his
mouth. Mama had made baked beans with molasses for
supper, and he was enjoying a hearty meal, smiling as
he tasted warm food after a day of hauling timber from
the woods with Jacob.

Lidda forced the words out. "The women, Papa, the

accused women—Tituba and Goody Osborne and Goody Good." She refused to use the word "witches," as if it somehow gave veracity to the accusations that they were servants of the Devil. Suddenly, an uneasy heat began in her stomach. *Not now, oh, please, not now!*

"The witches have been taken to Boston," Jacob said. "They will be jailed there, as they should be, and will be tried later."

"Why, son, how know you this?" Papa set down his spoon, looking longingly at the beans cooked in molasses.

"I hear things. I go about the town and talk to people at Ingersoll's tavern."

Because Mama did not approve of taverns, Lidda knew that Papa probably could not go about quite as freely as Jacob could. She stopped eating, all appetite gone, as the familiar but dreaded heat sizzled up her chest bones, seized her throat, and edged up her face and head. Her thoughts began to race inside, faster than snow hurled before the wind. She could see the three women—one so old she was literally bedridden; the other ill clothed and possibly mad; and the other, her friend—jolting in an open cart, exposed to snow and

111

chill winds, with only a small blanket to protect them—unless they rode in a stagecoach—sliding back and forth on the bench together, the hard wood rubbing their backsides raw—some rotten straw on the floor, the stench of earlier passengers and their sickness rising and pressing into their nostrils until they gagged—and then the jail, with no beds to sleep on, probably mounds of rat-infested piles of hay with foul odors—

Suddenly Lidda jumped up from the table, muttered an excuse about feeling ill, and ran out to the privy through the darkness, slamming the door behind her. An icy wind blew against the thin walls, knifing through the cracks. Even though she was without her cloak, Lidda barely felt the cold, for she was burning up with heat.

It had started in the core of her body, as always, rushing over her like a summer storm, only this storm did not bring welcome relief and healing rain; it brought anger, fear, and a wash of bright red in front of her eyes.

Lidda sat on the privy seat, holding her hands to her head and rocking back and forth. *I am not mad, I am not mad, this is something different, not madness.* She pounded the wood of the privy seat in her rage, daring it to contradict her, to say she was not mad.

She had not been able to say the word before, afraid of what it meant, of what the word might hold.

"Stop!" she screamed. "Leave me ALONE!" The wind swept her words out through the walls, carrying them over the frozen fields with only one solitary fox to hear, who stopped with pricked ears at the sounds of desperation and panic.

Lidda, Lidda, girl, crooned the internal voice. *I promise you are not going mad.*

At the same time the words flooded into her, the faint outline of Lucian appeared on the wall, lounging comfortably, feet planted, bare arms crossed over his chest.

"I cannot stand this anymore," Lidda cried, turning from the image that refused to fade, like some spot on a linen shirt which could not be scrubbed away. Squeezing her eyes shut, Lidda rocked back and forth on the seat, sobbing brokenheartedly. *I cannot live this way, rushing out to the privy each time I have an attack. What is* wrong *with me? Is it something I ate? Oh, how I wish it were something I ate, then I would know what to do.*

It is not something you ate, girl. It is given to you to see me. I know things few mortals do and have seen things few mortals have. You should be honored by my presence, Lidda.

The figure on the wall gestured nobly with his right hand. His silver eyes gleamed. Somehow, though her eyes were shut, she could see him, as if he were imprinted on the inside of her closed eyes.

Lidda stopped sobbing and pressed the hem of her dress to her eyes. The heat was receding now—her head did not feel as if it might burst into flames—and the cold locked around her arms and bare hands like a pitiless enemy.

"Honored?" She shivered.

Yes, honored. Ask me anything. I have knowledge beyond your wildest dreams, you poor child, stuck in this backwater of a town.

"Where do you come from?" Lidda breathed.

There was an answering silence, then something that sounded almost like a cough, and a muted reply: *That does not matter. You do not need to know that.*

"Then what *can* you tell me . . . Lucian?"

I do not come in the form of a cat or a dog or a pathetic, feeble yellow bird! I come to you as I am—full of power and beauty, magic and knowledge. Again I say, you should be honored.

"If you are powerful, Lucian, then do something

to help me!" Lidda sat straighter on the cold boards, shivering.

What do you desire?

"To be warm. For my family not to think me mad. For protection from this witch-fever. To be free of all of this."

A sudden pulse of warm air circled around her, beating back the freezing air, even warming the boards beneath her bottom. Her cold, crinkled petticoats and skirt rustled slightly, as if a July wind had moved them. Lidda's hands unclenched as a warm and delightful breeze passed over her.

Warmth is easy. Thoughts are more difficult.

Lidda let out a sigh. It was true what Lucian had said; he was not torturing her, he was helping her. Why was she resisting him so fiercely?

Yes, Lidda, I agree.

She sensed his beautiful head nodding and a small smile playing about his lips. Rising, she shook out her skirts and hurried back to the house, feeling very different than before when she had rushed out through the cold dark.

As Lidda took her seat on the bench, Susannah opened her mouth. "What took you so long, sister? I vow, you spend more time in the privy than anyone else in this house! We were just about to send Charity to see if you had slipped on the ice!"

"I did not slip and I did not fall." Lidda took up her spoon and pretended to eat, pushing the beans about her plate.

"Jacob," Susannah continued, losing interest in her sister, "you heard in the tavern that there are five girls, no, six who are afflicted now. It is spreading, and I wonder how many more will come forward, accusing the witches?"

Mama rocked Thomas back and forth in her arms, holding out her right hand in a warding gesture. "No witches shall enter this household. I dare them to try!" Her eyes glittered, and her hand clenched and unclenched.

"Why, wife, you sound fierce," Papa said.

"I am, husband! This is a plague, a trial of our town, and this house shall not be cursed! We will start by reading the Bible more during the day—not just for morning and evening prayers—with all of us praying for the witches to be caught and exposed."

At the same time that Lidda rebelled at the thought of more prayers—*useless things*—a lump rose in her throat. Could it work? If she joined in, mended her skirts, helped more with the cooking and cleaning and kept Thomas from crying, would it make a difference? Just yesterday, Papa had read to them Bible verses from the book of Jeremiah about the balm in Gilead; it was a holy ointment that healed all hurts and wounds. Was there balm in Gilead for her? Could she ever be an ordinary girl with an ordinary life?

You will have to choose what you want, girl, and I hope you make the right choice.

I just don't want to be so . . . different, Lidda said silently. But this time there was no answer, and Lidda rose hastily to help wash dishes and put them away. She sat obediently while Papa read from the Bible but felt the words bouncing off her shoulders like hailstones. They seemed to make no sense to her at all.

With one sharp look, Jacob handed a lit candle to Lidda, and she and Charity tromped upstairs to their bedroom, the flame wavering in the breeze. Lidda thought Charity's back seemed small and bowed, as if she carried too heavy a burden. She felt a wave of protectiveness, and when they reached their bedroom, she set down the candle.

"What is wrong, sister?"

"I should be asking *you* that question!" Charity whirled around, grabbing Lidda about her middle. "What is wrong? You can tell me, tell Charity who loves you best of all."

Lidda stood mutely, grasping the back of her sister, wishing, yearning to tell.

Charity coaxed, "I know something is bothering you. I see your face flush red before you run out to the privy. What are you hiding? Are you ill?"

Lidda burst into racking sobs. She could never tell Charity what was wrong—Lucian had threatened her if she told anyone.

"Oh, Charity, I am—I am unwell. I am so frightened about Tituba. . . ." She coughed and gulped, trying to talk and shuddering instead. No more words came out, only the violent shaking of her body against her sister's. Even if she had tried to tell Charity, it seemed she could not. Something or *someone* prevented her.

"There, there," Charity crooned, as if singing to baby Thomas. "Let me help, dear one."

Charity undid the buttons on Lidda's bodice, took it off, and laid it on the clothes chest; then she untied

Lidda's skirt and petticoats and set them down neatly. She tried to retie the strings on Lidda's cap but could not because her sister's chin was trembling so.

"There, get into bed; Susannah will be up soon. Sleep, dear one, sleep."

Like a five-year-old, Lidda obediently climbed into bed, pulling the covers up to her chin as tears ran down her cold cheeks.

"There," Charity soothed, sitting on the bed and smoothing her sister's hair. "Sleep, sleep," and she began to hum a lullaby. As the notes surrounded her, Lidda became still at last, closed her eyes, and drifted into a dark sleep where beautiful shadows chased her, whispering her name, and a face beyond human beauty grinned and beckoned to her.

15

THE NEXT MORNING, LIDDA WORKED harder than usual, tidying the chilled rooms, rocking Thomas, and helping Mama prepare the vegetables and haunch of beef for the midday meal.

Even Susannah gazed at Lidda with approval. "This is the way to behave, sister. You see how much you can accomplish when you apply yourself." She gave a small and private smile as she bent over Papa's thick socks, darning a hole.

"Mama?" Lidda asked. "Do you need my help now? May I go visit Ann Putnam to see how she fares? I have not seen her since the examination of Goody Good in the meetinghouse. . . ."

Susannah broke in, eyes gleaming. "Ann fell on the floor with the others, their arms akimbo and their legs frozen and faces twisted into impossible expressions!

What else could it be but witches? No person could will their body that way!"

Mama murmured her assent. "Yes, Lidda, go and visit that poor girl. Perhaps you can aid or comfort her in some way."

But it was not aid or comfort that Lidda had in mind. It was truth that she sought. Now that Betty Parris had been sent away to relatives in nearby Salem Town, Lidda had no one to talk to—whom she trusted—about what was happening in the village. Ann was the only one she could think of, but she was not sure she trusted her at all—not after seeing her fall to the floor in the meeting-house and writhe about with the other girls. It seemed the only one she could trust right now was . . . Lucian, odd as that seemed.

Quite right, girl.

Wrapping her cloak about her, Lidda walked the short distance to the Putnam house, pausing before the rather grand door. She was not sure whether this was a good time to visit, for so many in this house-hold had been afflicted by torments: Mercy Lewis, their servant, had suffered several fits, as had Ann her-self, and Mary Walcott, who lived with them. Lidda knocked softly on the door.

Ann opened it, looking as if she had just come through a windstorm. She was a small, compact girl with dark hair and bright eyes, who usually was fastidiously neat. Not today, with her linen cap askew and hair trailing down her flushed cheeks.

"Oh, Lidda, come in, do, our household is a bit confused at the moment, you will have to forgive us."

Entering the kitchen with its roaring fire, Lidda noticed that Mistress Putnam was nowhere to be seen. Mercy Lewis, a spare girl with a dribble under her nose, was stirring soup in a pot over the fire. She nodded to Lidda and said, "This is a sad household, a sad and afflicted household." She pressed one hand to her forehead.

"Come in by the fire." Ann tugged on Lidda's hand as a sudden scream sounded from the room above. Ann flinched.

"Who is that?"

"It sounds like Mama. Oh, Lord, let it not be Mama!"

"Hurry," Mercy said, charging up the stairs ahead of them. "We must help her."

They ran behind her into the bedroom, where

Mistress Putnam lay on a fine bed. Nearby, Mister Putnam held one of her hands, pressing it to his lips and praying—

"Dear Lord, spare us this affliction, take all evil creatures away from my wife, I pray thee, Lord, defend us from evil. . . ."

Mistress Putnam's head swung from side to side, and her feet thrashed beneath the covers, making them jump and ripple. Lidda stepped back, afraid. This did not look like someone making up an attack—this looked real. Sweat beaded the woman's face, and tears gushed from her eyes as she moaned, "Go away, get thee behind me, Satan, go away, I am a good woman, a good Bible woman. . . ."

Mercy went up to the other side of the bed and took her hand, praying that the Lord would spare her this trial.

Suddenly Mistress Putnam sat up, thrusting her hands toward the window. "Get away from me, Goody Corey, let you not be outside my window. Go away!"

"What is it, my dear love, whom do you see?" her husband begged.

His wife lay back, pressing her hands to her chest and

moaning. "She is sitting on me, crushing my chest. . . ." She began to cough and gasp for breath. "And Goody Nurse, too . . ."

Mister Putnam fell to his knees as did Ann and Mercy, chanting the Lord's Prayer: "Our Father, who art in heaven, hallowed be Thy name . . ."

Almost choking, Mistress Putnam raised her head and cried out, "No, get thee behind me, Satan, I will not sign my name in your red book, I will not!"

Lidda stared at all of them. They had run mad, mad as winter cows let out of their imprisoning barn. There was no stopping them.

As the Lord's Prayer drew to a finish, the woman sank back onto the bedstead and drew in a deep breath.

"There, my love, there." Her husband patted her hand, then wiped her brow with a kerchief. "You will be all right, see, the Lord's words have brought you back to us."

"Praises be," Mercy intoned, and Ann joined in. Lidda did not. What was there to praise in this display? Chills ran up and down her body—the room felt icy and empty of any human comfort.

Ann stepped forward, wiping the tears from her

mother's cheeks. "All is well now, Mama, sleep, sleep."

"The Lord is merciful," her husband said fervently, "slow to anger and rich in kindness. Thank you, Ann and Mercy. Stay with her while I go about town to tell what has happened to my wife. A new affliction in our house—that makes four! Guard her!" he commanded, and ran out of the room.

Lidda had no doubt that he would visit the tavern to tell what had just befallen his wife. She shivered again, her stomach clutching in painfully. The storm that was roiling over Salem Village had just gained new energy and direction, new ferocity.

Lidda leaned against the wall and watched as Ann's mother fell into an exhausted sleep. Yet—for all that she had endured—her face had a rosy hue and did not have the wasted look one might expect after such an attack. For a moment, when Mistress Putnam's legs had kicked and flailed, Lidda thought she caught an expression of excitement in the curved lines around her mouth. And she thought she had seen Mistress Putnam peering out at them from under her half-closed eyelids, as if to test their reactions.

"You see how it is, Lid," Ann whispered, "how she

has been attacked and ravaged by the witches' specters and the Devil." She clenched her fists. "But Papa will find them—if anyone can! He is like a dog sinking its teeth into a bull's nose. He will never let go until they arrest those who are harming Mama."

Lidda hesitated. "We saw in the meetinghouse that you were oppressed, too, Ann. Was it like this?"

The girl shook her head. "It was different. She is much noisier!" Her laugh was suddenly shrill. "I have fits when I am with the other girls—you saw me when they were questioning Tituba and the other two witches."

"The other witches," Mercy intoned, looking pale and drawn.

Because Lidda was afraid that Mercy might fall to the floor in a fit matching Mistress Putnam's, she quickly asked, "Mercy, could you bring some cider up to the bedroom, please? I think when your mistress wakes she would like something to drink."

Sullenly Mercy trailed out of the room, thumping loudly down the stairs.

Lidda continued, asking the question she most wanted the answer to: "What did it feel like, Ann, when Goody Good was being examined?"

"Oh, like a wind passing over us, each by each, chilling us and freezing our limbs—as if ice were being poured into my bones! It was awful, Lidda!"

Mistress Putnam's eyelashes fluttered as she stirred in her sleep.

"Hush, we are talking too loudly." Gently, Ann smoothed her mother's hair away from her flushed cheeks.

"But, Ann . . ." Lidda remembered the two of them in summertime, walking through the meadows, searching for wild strawberries. The girl had always been sensible, if a bit bossy, and sometimes she was even merry. It was a welcome change from what girls were meant to be like in Salem—straitlaced, good at household chores, attentive in church, soft of manner, and obedient. Always obedient. And yet? At the first examination Ann had twitched her skirt in a decisive gesture. Immediately she and the other girls had fallen to the floor and begun their "fits."

What could be driving her to make such dire accusations, to put so many in peril? And even more, why make it up?

"Could you stop it, do you think, when a fit comes over you?"

Ann paused. "I do not know. It is almost like when

a cow gets sick. First one does in the meadow, then another—they seem to pass it from one to another. It is like that."

Lidda sucked in a breath, the words sinking into her. A whisper of a voice said, *Just so, Lidda.*

She had trouble keeping the horror from her face. This was an admission, a description of their afflictions that was very different from the descriptions of the other girls. Ann spoke of something they shared with each other, caught from one another. But who could she tell this to, and who would believe her? There must be others in Salem who did not believe what was happening, who did not think that Goody Osborne, confined to her bed, rode about on a broomstick hurting children. There had to be a way to expose these lies without being accused herself of being a witch.

What shall I do, Lucian? she pleaded, but there was no answer, just an uneasy silence filled with the feverish breathing of Mistress Putnam and the sound of an icy wind against the clapboards. The pitiless sound reminded her of the vision she'd had earlier of the village, with unplanted fields and houses slumping in disrepair. How could one girl stop what was happening? It would be like standing in a field against a thunderstorm, holding out her arms to stop the whirling winds, rain, and lightning.

16

MISERABLE. EVERYTHING WAS MISERABLE.
The cold pulled in like the strings on her stays. Her lips
were chapped, the skin on her fingers flaked at the ends,
and her toes in the too-wide boots stubbed against the
frozen leather each time she went out to the barn to feed
the chickens.

Lucian muttered within. *What a useless village this is.
What a dismal climate! I am protected from the cold, but I
can feel how it bends your body to its rigid necessities.*

He was right, of course, but how did he know that
her body felt bent and bound by the cold? How could
he sense what was happening to her? Lidda pressed one
hand to the middle of her body, over the bulk of her
cloak. Was it *here* that he lived? Or—she moved her
hand farther up, over her heart—*here*? His voice seemed
to echo and resonate throughout her entire body when

he spoke, and at the same time there was a burning feeling near her core. If this was being a companion, she would hate to see what it would be like to have Lucian as her enemy.

You would indeed, girl.

She could not decide if she felt reassured by his comments or unnerved, but she rather thought she welcomed Lucian's voice by now, even when it seemed a bit threatening. He was becoming known, familiar . . . hers.

Walking swiftly to get warm, Lidda headed toward the barn in back, grasping the door with one hand. Mama had told her to let the chickens out into the sunshine, as it was a day without wind or snowfall, calm enough for Papa and Jacob to haul more wood from the forest with their mare. When Lidda opened the door to the barn, the chickens clustered at the entrance, dazed by the bright sun, and then carefully, hesitantly, like people who have forgotten how to walk, they eased themselves out onto the patch of trampled snow.

Scooping her fingers into the bag full of hard kernels, Lidda scattered the corn over the glittering white. Squawking and clucking, the chickens rushed toward the yellow corn, pushing against one another, one almost diving through another's legs to get at the food.

Lidda laughed to see the chickens scrambling over and under each other, their necks outstretched, and beaks pecking, pecking . . . like the witch-fever girls, she thought.

Just like the witch-fever girls, except that is too kind a word. I call them the murder girls.

Lidda sucked in a breath. *Will it come to that?* she asked silently, but there was no answer. Suddenly she heard someone walking on the road past the front of the house. Adjusting her cloak and smoothing her hair, she went out to see who it was. A woman wearing a tall black hat and a swirling cloak strode purposefully down the lane.

When a sudden wind blew up, her cloak lifted, revealing a bright red waistcoat with colored embroidery on it. Lidda gasped. Never had she seen anything so beautiful, so vivid! What courage it must take to dress in this fashion, in a village that made a religion of dowdiness, restraint, and dull colors.

Lidda bent her head and murmured, "Good day to you," to the woman, who paused, midstride, and answered, "Good day to you, child, and it is good with this bright sunshine." She spread her arms out to the sky, as if lifting it up single-handedly, and smiled at Lidda.

She beamed at her. This person seemed like someone from a foreign land—smiles, a red waistcoat, and walking with such assurance and direction, almost like a man!

"I am Goody Bishop, and I think I know this house. Your father is Mister Johnson, the carpenter, is he not?"

Lidda nodded. "That he is, and I am Lidda, his daughter, the disappointing one, who dreams too much and wishes to dance under the moon."

Where had *those* words come from?

Goody Bishop laughed heartily. "Then you and I shall get along just fine, for I, too, like to dance outside. At my tavern, we play shuffleboard and drink strong cider late at night. Do you think you would like that, Lidda?" The woman's eyes gleamed with amusement.

"I would," Lidda answered. "But I could never get away to visit your tavern; my mama would not let me, nor my papa."

"No, I suppose they would not. And in these dangerous times, we must all be more careful. Now, I must be going to Mister Shattuck's house." She waved a wrapped package. "I have some things for him to dye, little bits and fragments of lace." She paused and said confidingly, "I must do something to cheer myself up in this village, and to make my clothing cheerful as well." Then she was gone, striding down the street and turning onto a path that led to a brown house.

Lidda threw her arms wide, sucking in the air left in Goody Bishop's wake. There was a scent to her—of cider, of smoke, of something baking—a kind, alive scent that she wished she could stuff into a bag to keep for herself. It reminded her of Tituba, who she suddenly missed intensely. Was she warm enough in her jail cell, and did they give her enough to eat? She doubted it. And just as bad was what she had heard from Jacob, that all of the accused were chained in irons.

When Lidda went back inside the house, Susannah rounded on her fiercely. "I saw you talking to Goody Bishop! She is not a good sort of woman, not good at all. You should not be talking to her!"

Lidda bridled. "And why not? Who made you the judge of my actions and what is proper and not proper?"

Mama nodded from her seat. "Lidda is right, Susannah, it is for me to tell her what is proper. But . . ." She paused, settling Thomas on her other breast.

"Susannah is right. Goody Bishop is not a godly woman. She is known to have loud, public arguments with her husband—in the past she did.

"And," Mama continued, "she keeps late hours at her tavern, misleading the youth of our village."

Cider and shuffleboard. Sinful activities indeed.

"Shhh!" Lidda said, and Susannah flared up again.

"Don't you shush me, sister! I am your elder, wiser and more cautious than you."

Lidda bent her head, unwilling to engage in yet another argument with Susannah. But a smile tugged at the edges of her mouth as she remembered Goody Bishop sailing along the street like a ship on the ocean, cape fluttering, with a glimpse of bright red cloth beneath the black cloak. It seemed to promise happiness, rebellion, things of the flesh, and parts of the Bible that Mama would never let her read. Lidda wanted to be friends with Goody Bishop but knew her family would never allow it. Goody was too free in her ways, and especially in this time of discord and fear, Lidda could not reach out to her.

I like that woman, Lucian said. *I like her spirit.*

"So do I," whispered Lidda.

She reminds me of you. His voice was tender and amused, and Lidda held on to the words as she imagined herself wearing a red waistcoat under a swirling black cloak, striding down the street like a man.

17

LIDDA KNOCKED ON THE DOOR TO THE Putnams' house, shifting the steaming jug from one hand to the other. Mama had made a thick, flavorful beef broth to help Mistress Putnam recover from her attacks, although after seeing the look of excitement in the woman's eyes, Lidda suspected they were not attacks at all but something far different. But she knew that Mama would never believe her if she tried to tell her that.

She knocked again. There was no answer. Softly she pushed the door inward, and it swung on its hinges with a faint groan. It was strangely quiet inside; the house seemed empty. No bustle, no Mercy Lewis going up and down stairs with jugs of hot water for her mistress; no one tending the fire in the big room or baking bread in the wall oven. The other children in the family seemed absent, or perhaps they were busy doing chores else-where in the house or outside.

Lidda saw that the fire was sinking down upon itself, and quickly she shut the door, so as not to let in any more of the freezing air. For some reason, she did not call out, either to Ann or to Mercy. Drifting like a shadow, she headed for the half-closed door to the room opposite the kitchen and hid behind it. Someone was inside—she could hear whispering.

There—that high, quick voice belonged to Ann. It was followed by the lower, slower sound of Mercy, and then another girl, who she thought might be Elizabeth Hubbard, and one other, who could be Mary Walcott, who also lived here.

" . . . we can say we saw his specter," said Ann.

"At night, outside our window . . ." That was Mercy's breathless response.

"He could press down on our chests . . ." The words followed hard on Mercy's reply.

"His specter—but . . ." The voice lowered. "How will we know what he wore?"

"It matters not" came the unknown speaker. "As long as we agree . . ." The voices dropped, and Lidda missed what they were saying.

Then Ann spoke. "If all of us say the same thing . . ."
A flutter of excited sounds clustered together like birds.

" . . . all of us accusing him . . . he will not have . . ."
A pause, a quick beat . . .

". . . a chance," they said together.

Lidda sucked in a breath, tucked her arms close to her side, and stepped quietly backward toward the front door, still holding the jug of warm beef broth.

Gritting her teeth, she slipped through the door and staggered out onto the front step. Where to go? And who were they about to accuse? Hugging the jug to her body as if to cradle its warmth, Lidda set out for home, wondering what she could do.

After supper, as Papa lit his long clay pipe with a coal from the fire, Lidda watched him suck in the smoke, letting it trickle slowly out of the sides of his mouth. He sighed deeply, appearing to find comfort in the familiar ritual, and stretched out his boots to the fire.

"No more accusations today, husband," Mama said.

"That is a relief," said Jacob, trying vainly to light his pipe. The tobacco smoldered and flared; smoke rose for a second and then subsided.

Lidda smiled briefly, but the scene she had heard

earlier had left her almost frozen inside, unable to decide what to do.

"I am sure there will be more accusations," Susannah said with satisfaction. "They are not stopping with two old women and the foreign-born slave—though Mistress Putnam accused Goody Corey and Goody Nurse. And Ann Jr. accused little Dorcas Good. I vow there are more witches in this village for certain!"

Papa nodded, but Lidda noticed new lines of worry on his forehead. She wondered what he truly thought about these "witches." Over on the bench, Charity was knitting in the dim firelight; and then she exclaimed, putting down her small needles, "There is not enough light, Mama! I will do more tomorrow."

"All right, child. We are tired by what is happening in the village, and I vow a good night's sleep is what we all need."

How can I sleep knowing what I know now? Lidda thought. There was no answering voice within, only silence.

"Papa," she said hesitantly, moving one hand onto the table.

He looked over at her and smiled. "Yes, Lidda?"

"Papa, what would happen if it could be proven that the girls are ly—" Susannah coughed suspiciously, but Lidda pressed on. "Lying, Papa?"

His head snapped back, and he took his pipe out of his mouth. "That is a dire thing to say, child. Wherever did you get such an idea? People could not invent tales like this!" He inserted the pipe into his mouth again and inhaled deeply.

Lidda watched the smoke disappear into the dark overhead. "But how do we *know* they are telling the truth, Papa?"

He set down his pipe and sighed. "Ah, Lidda, Lidda, child, you think you know more than the magistrates—educated men? More than Magistrate Jonathan Hathorne and Mister Corwin?"

Lidda ducked her head, fiddling with her skirt. "No, Papa," she murmured, "it is just that . . . what if?"

"Lidda!" exclaimed Mama. "This is dangerous talk! You must not let anyone in meeting or elsewhere hear you speaking such nonsense. It would cause trouble for all of us!"

"But, Mama . . ." She could not stop herself. "Does *everyone* in the village believe what the girls are saying?"

Mama pushed back her hair and sighed. "I think there are one or two people who are protesting, who do not believe . . . but we do not side with them, daughter, not at all!" She tapped her fingers on the table with each word, until at the end, with "not at all!," her hand thumped on the wood for emphasis.

Charity plucked at Lidda's sleeve and murmured, "Time for bed, sister."

"Yes, indeed," Papa agreed, rising and dusting off his breeches. "The coming days will be long, and the next set of examinations will come soon."

"But, Papa–" Lidda stopped as Charity seized her arm, tugging her toward the staircase, saying, "Hush, no more!"

As they tramped up the stairs, four words sounded inside Lidda—

A valiant try, girl.

18

❦

THE NEXT EVENING, THEY HEARD A DOOR
slamming with an audible *thunk!* down the road.
Susannah jumped up from the bench where she had
been mending and peered out the front window.

"It is Reverend Parris's house! Someone just went
inside—couldn't quite see who it was, a man, I think."
Susannah wiped frantically at the frost on the windowpane.

Lidda came over behind her, seeing a burst of light,
then darkness as their neighbor's door closed. "Who is
visiting?"

"It looks like Reverend Deodat Lawson." Jacob
walked over to the two girls. "I was at Ingersoll's tavern
earlier when he was interviewing Mary Walcott."

"Tell me, brother!" Susannah jigged up and down.
"Tell me what happened."

"She pulled up her sleeve to show him the recent marks of the Devil's teeth on her wrist!" Jacob's voice rose in wonder and excitement.

"Bitten on her skin?" Susannah shrieked. "That is what the Devil does? Bite innocent maidens?"

Lidda was not sure how innocent Mary Walcott was. Did she not hear Mary's voice that day when listening to the girls plotting at Mister Putnam's house?

Mama let out a long sigh. "It is worse than we ever could have imagined. Where will this stop, my husband, where will it stop?" She turned to him, clutching Thomas to her breast.

He touched her shoulder gently. "There are good people in the village working against this plague, dear one, we can be confident about that!"

No, we cannot. Not confident about "good" or anything else, sir.

Lidda backed away from the window and settled near the fire. She poked the logs with a tool and was rewarded with a shower of bright sparks and flames shooting up the chimney.

Worse, it was getting worse.

That surprises you, girl?

Susannah threw on her cloak and asked permission. "Papa, may I go visit Abigail? I might be of help to them. . . ." She skittered toward the door, awaiting Papa's response.

"I suppose you can, daughter, but come home soon, do not stay out late."

Mama shivered. "Who knows what might be lurking abroad during the dark of the night, husband?"

"I will go with her, though it is a short walk to the Reverend's door." Papa threw on his cloak, lit a lantern, and shepherded Susannah outside.

Lidda tapped her foot restlessly against the hearthstones. What was happening? Who would be accused next? She had not yet heard the results of the girls' plotting and who they would name. Could she do anything at all about it?

Help, she said silently. *We need help, Lucian!*

Use your mind, girl. You are intelligent and not without courage. Think of something.

But staring into the orange-and-red flames, listening to Charity's knitting needles clicking nearby, nothing came to Lidda. She thought, *If I only knew who was next, I could write them a note and tell them to saddle up their horse and escape! Or I could advise them to go for a long visit to some relative far away, immediately!*

Time stretched, and shortened, and stretched again as they waited for Papa and Susannah to return, which they finally did just before bedtime, slamming through the door on a blast of frigid air.

"Whew!" Papa said, hanging up his cloak and sitting heavily on the bench. His face was distressed, with worry lines sagging about his mouth. He reached up, mussed his hair vigorously with one hand, and sighed again. "I never," he said. "Never. In all my life. Hope to see anything like that again."

Even Susannah was quiet, but with a sense of bubbling excitement and anticipation. Clearly she was waiting for Papa to finish.

"Oh, Mama, you should have seen Abigail when Reverend Lawson came to visit."

"What did she do?" Mama laid Thomas in his cradle, giving him a last fond pat.

"She ran about the room shouting, 'Whish, whish, whish!' as if she had no knowledge that we were there, or that her uncle had visitors. And then—"

Papa broke in. "She seized logs from the fireplace—burning logs—and heaved them out onto the floor. I leaped forward to kick them back into the fireplace!"

"Reverend Lawson examined her hands, and they were not burned. How could that be?" Susannah waved her hands dramatically in front of her face. "How could that girl not be burned? It must be . . ." Her voice dropped. "The Devil, his minions, or witches."

Hmph! Lucian snorted. *If you move fast enough, you will not be burned.*

Lidda lifted her head, reassured to have Lucian telling her what had really happened. But that did not matter in the end; what mattered was the interpretation people put on it.

The lies they tell about it, you mean.

Susannah paused, pushing back her linen cap. "It was most dramatic, almost . . ." She pressed one finger against her mouth. "Holy and instructive."

Nonsense!

"Nonsense! This makes no sense at all. Why would Abigail do such a thing, take such a risk?" Lidda exclaimed.

"Who knows how the Devil works, child?" Papa

answered wearily. "Who knows? Never have we seen anything like this in our village before. We are possessed!"

Mama thunked her hands down on the table. "I am frightened, John."

"We all are, wife. Here." Papa stood, handed out the lit candles for them to take to their bedrooms, and said, "Let the good Lord protect us and guide us this night, may we be spared all evil visitations, and may the morning dawn bright and clear with no harm near us."

"Amen," they murmured as they went their separate ways.

You might just as well say "Whish, whish, whish!" for all the good this will do.

"Hush!" Lidda whispered, and Charity turned on the stairs, giving her a wide-eyed look.

"Hush, who, sister? Who are you talking to? I vow, sometimes it seems as if there is a third person following us about, and you are talking to her. Or him."

Careful, Lidda . . .

"I want the whole village to hush, Charity, to stop its noise and falsehoods," Lidda said.

"You think the girls lie, Lidda? Do you know that for certain?"

"I do. They are making this up, sister, and I know not what to do about it." Lidda caught her breath on a sob and plunged upstairs into the dark, getting into bed without undressing at all.

What difference did it make whether she was dressed or undressed, clean or unclean? She was just a fourteen-year-old girl in the village of Salem, without power, except the power to tell truth from lies. And that made her even more alone than ever.

19

"WELL, DEAR ONES." PAPA STOOD BY THE door, wrapped up against the cold. "It is time to go. Reverend Deodat Lawson will be preaching today, and I am sure he will have something to say about this plague that is upon us."

"Plague," said Susannah in a satisfied tone.

Lidda pressed her lips together to keep from responding.

Susannah eyed her suspiciously, as if she knew the rebellious thoughts coursing through her sister's mind.

All Lidda could do was stamp her foot upon the floor impatiently, enough to make everyone look at her but not bad enough to earn a reproof from Mama.

Charity stepped close and plucked at her cloak. "Lid? Are you ready? Are you ill? Do you want me to go with you to the privy?"

"No!" Lidda lashed out, thrusting Charity's hand away. "Stop asking me questions! Please," she added in an undertone, wishing to erase the hurt look on her sister's face.

Stop trying to appease her, Lidda. She will never understand you.

With a great effort of will, Lidda kept herself from shouting "Hush!"

Then Lucian began to sing a lilting song. Lidda felt the notes slide down her arms and legs, and circle up through her head; they had colors like sky birds— orange, yellow, blue, purple, and a kind of green almost beyond imagining, like the tiniest, brightest, newest leaf just before it unfurls, all curled in upon itself. That kind of green.

> *Once there was a maiden young*
> *with a hey-nonny-nonny*
> *who fell in love*
> *with a hey-nonny-nonny*
> *and her dear brave boy*
> *with a hey-nonny-nonny*
> *touched her on her breast*
> *with a hey-nonny-ho—*

Now Lidda's foot began to tap the floor, over and over to the sound of the cheery melody. Of course, Mama would be horrified at the improper words and would scrub them from Lidda's mind if she could, just the way she threw water on the floor once it was spring and scrubbed it with a brush . . . a brush . . . a brush—

> *and he brushed his lips*
> *with a hey-nonny-nonny*
> *against her sweet full lips*
> *with a hey-nonny-ho*
> *sweet as two ripe cherries—*

"Lidda, I declare you get worse each day! What are your feet doing? Surely you are not *dancing*?" Susannah exclaimed.

"Oh, no, sister," Lidda answered quickly. "I am just impatient to get to the service."

"That is better, then." Susannah tugged at Lidda's hand, dragging her to the open door. Outside, their neighbors streamed past on the way to the meetinghouse to hear Reverend Lawson.

That very unpleasant man, never touched by beauty,

with his wretched red scalp showing through. Why does he not hide in a barn?

Lidda yelped with laughter, then, at the startled expressions on her sisters' faces, drew the hood farther up on her head and strode out the door. Her feet stepped onto the path, seemingly without her directing them. Lidda saw her dull, brown, serviceable boots marching over the hard snow. If she had her way, she would be dancing along the street in a red embroidered waistcoat like Goody Bishop, throwing her arms out to the sky and calling down those colored notes of the raucous, entirely unsuitable but oh-so-delicious song that Lucian was singing.

She could sense him twirling inside, dipping and rising, then bending in a graceful arc. Biting her lower lip, Lidda looked at Charity's beloved face, her frightened eyes, and tried to still the dancing within.

Oh, go on, girl, you want to dance!

No, not here, not now, she answered silently.

Charity did not try to talk to her anymore but stayed close, leaning against her as they headed toward the meetinghouse. Lidda followed Susannah and Mama to the women's side of the building and took a seat. It was all she could do to keep herself on the hard cold bench. Her feet kept wanting to point and dance; her legs wanted—oh, how they wanted!—to jump and twirl through the doleful room to the sunny outdoors.

This room has not the right kind of darkness, Lidda. I prefer the velvety blackness of a night sky.

Lidda had just enough presence of mind left to grind the fingers of her left hand into her thigh, making it burn and ache enough to stifle any response.

Reverend Lawson stood up, stretched out his arms to them in what might be a beseeching manner or a hectoring manner, and raised his voice so all could hear.

"Oh, villagers, what dire judgment has come upon you? How it strikes my heart to hear of your trials and persecutions by the Devil, the fountain of malice. Indeed, the Devil is come down in great wrath upon you in Salem!" The service went on, his words droning out the psalm when the Reverend was suddenly interrupted as Abigail Williams rose from her seat.

"Now stand up and name your text."

The Reverend gaped at her. Never before had a young girl interrupted a sacred service; it was unheard of. But he named the text he had been preaching from, and Abigail replied smartly, "It is a long text."

Dreadfully long and boring!

Reverend Lawson struggled to regain his composure, patting his hair and clearing his throat. Lucian fell silent for a moment, but wicked laughter bubbled inside Lidda, especially when the Reverend exhorted them to "Arm, arm, arm yourselves against Satan's might!"

After some time another villager, Mistress Pope, spoke up. "Now there is enough of that!"

Lidda giggled, trying to hide her laughter from Mama, who gave her a fierce look of rebuke. Luckily her mother could not see Lidda's boots tapping the floorboards beneath her skirt, itching to dance, to do anything to get out of this horrid meetinghouse where the noise continued to boil like an unwatched pot.

While people nearby tried to pull her down, Abigail stood and cried out, "There is Goody Corey sitting on the beam, suckling a yellow bird between her fingers!"

People craned their necks, trying to get a glimpse and talking loudly about whether this might be the same one that Tituba had seen—clearly a devil in disguise.

Ann Putnam jumped up, saying, "I see a little bird on your hat over there!"

Again, the villagers peered at the Reverend's hat hanging on the wall, and some called out that they, too, could see the yellow bird. The noise rose in volume.

Lidda looked over at Ann, wondering what she was trying to do. With the new, sharper senses that Lucian had given her, she saw Ann's flushed, excited face—the satisfied eyes and mouth of someone who was finally being heard at last, finally being important.

Somehow Lawson continued to preach through the outcry and babbling voices, though Lidda could scarce hear him over the noise outside and within as Lucian continued to sing and chant in a way that drowned out the hectoring tones of the Reverend.

It was almost impossible to stay seated on the hard bench, torn between the joy rising within and her disgust at what was happening in the room. She wanted to leap to her feet and accuse Ann Putnam of lying and point her finger at Abigail Williams.

Do it, Lidda!

No, I cannot. They would name me as a witch next, you know that!

The only answer this time was the lilting inner song that erased all the ugliness in the room, that washed away the cruel deception. Her hands no longer obeyed her as they lifted up in the air; nor did her legs. Jumping up, she hurried through the raucous congregation, not even telling Charity that she felt ill. It would be an untruth, and there had been too much lying in this village. The truth was, she was not ill. She had never felt better in her life. She felt as if a bright stream of silver water were swirling inside of her, carrying words, dreams, and music with it. She felt powerful—capable, invincible—even beautiful.

Good girl, leave them all behind and dance.

Once she was outside the dark room, Lidda flung back the hated gray hood, pretending she wore a bright scarlet cloak instead, and danced down the frozen path with no one to see, holding her hands out to the light.

20

THE LAST DAYS FELT AS IF SOMEONE HAD thrown a black pall over the house. Everyone seemed to be in mourning, even the house. The windows were dull and gray, the floor lifeless; the fire simmered with a sullen glow. And all because she had had the boldness to leave services! Lidda had to endure endless lectures from Papa ("Never again, daughter!"); Mama ("You brought shame on us all!"); Susannah ("Why cannot I have a sister like other girls?"); even Charity had given her a searching look and pleaded with her never to do such a thing again. Only Jacob had said nothing, merely eyeing her over his pipe and shaking his head slowly from side to side.

It was a welcome relief when Susannah forgot to upbraid her and confided one morning, "Mary Warren is oppressed now, too, Lidda. She said the Devil wanted her to write in his red book!" Susannah sucked in a breath, clicking her teeth together. "His red book!" she repeated.

The madness grows.

Lidda nodded in response, and it was clear Susannah thought she was agreeing with her, for she repeated cheerfully, "His red book! What will happen next, I wonder?"

Let me guess—more lies?

Lidda pressed one hand to her middle in agreement and said, "Mama? I would like to go visit Mary Warren. It is sad that she lost her parents and now has to work as a servant in the Proctors' household."

"Mmm." Susannah frowned. "Should you be visiting that house, Lidda? Ann Putnam has accused Mistress Proctor, and I heard Mister Proctor thinks Mary is lying. Some say he even beat her."

"Then Mary Warren will need companionship and cheer," Lidda replied, tying the ribbons of her cloak. She was determined not to be stopped from getting away from her family, and the Proctors' house was far enough away so that she could walk off some of today's gloom.

Mama nodded. "You may go, Lidda, just do not stay too long. It will do you good to be seen about the village, so that people know there is nothing wrong with you. We have told our neighbors that you were sick the day you left church, and indeed . . ."

Lidda slipped out the door before Mama could finish, finding it impossible to listen anymore. *I was not sick*, Lidda told herself as she hurried down the path. *I was dancing and no one could see. It was heaven!*

Almost running, she headed toward the Proctors' tavern on the Ipswich Road, eager to get away from Thomas's cries, Susannah's complaints, even from Charity, who kept asking what was wrong and looking at her with warm, sympathetic eyes.

Sympathy. It undoes one, does it not? Those warm honeyed eyes . . .

If he only knew—but, of course he *did* know—how her eyes filled with tears when Charity put a hand on her arm, saying, "Please tell me what is wrong."

What is wrong! Lucian mocked, in an uncanny imitation of Charity's voice.

Stop it! You are not allowed to make fun of my sister!

My apologies, girl. I thought I was bringing you the power to see who lies and who does not—and you are correcting me like a preacher!

Lidda's shoulders sagged, and she held one hand to her middle, where the voice—once there, resonating—suddenly disappeared. She did not know how to answer Lucian or the strange emptiness within, so she walked faster to see if she could outwalk her unease.

After some time, she reached the pathway to Mister Proctor's house. It radiated a sense of comfort and welcome that was alien to their village, Lidda thought. When she knocked on the door, a harried-looking Mary opened it.

"May I come in?" Lidda asked.

The girl gestured toward the main room, where a fire burned and Mistress Proctor sat close to it, fidgeting with her russet skirt, clenching and unclenching her hands on the fabric.

"Good day, Mistress Proctor." Lidda made a slight bob to the young matron, who had a pale, queasy look.

"Mary, please fetch us some cider and biscuits," Mistress Proctor said, surprising Lidda that she would treat a young girl like her with such courtesy. "This is a dire end to winter, is it not?" the woman asked, pleating and unpleating her skirt.

Lidda gave her a quick glance, with the acute vision

she had acquired from having Lucian living within. She read unease and a deep anger in the tense lines about Mistress Proctor's mouth and the furrows in her brow. An indefinable smell rose from her clothing, a little like fear but containing something different—sour and acrid. Lidda paused, trying to tease out the meaning of it.

"Lidda?" Mistress Proctor put her hand on the girl's arm. "Are you well? You seem—far away and distressed, somehow."

Lidda waited for the raucous comment, the snide laughter, but there was only silence. It rocked her, made her feel uneven and unbalanced now that she was so used to Lucian's presence. Finally she stumbled over the words.

"I fear the news that your Mary is also afflicted, and I worry that you have been named by Ann Putnam, too."

"She is not *my* Mary," the woman muttered as the servant girl entered the room, bearing two mugs filled with hot cider and a plate of crisp brown biscuits. "And it will take more than another wild accusation from that Putnam girl to bring this family down!" Her chin jutted out as she said this.

Lidda caught a look in Mary's eyes when it seemed

no one was looking—a haunted and confused expression—and her shoulders hunched under her workaday dress.

"Mary," Lidda began, "please tell me what happened." She sipped the hot cider and let out a grateful sigh.

Mary tried to stand up straight and began. "It was a cold, moonlit night, and I could not sleep. I kept looking out the window, afraid of that great white moon staring in through the glass. It seemed like a huge eye.

"I could not sleep—I know not why. Prickles and shivers kept going up and down my body, as if someone were dragging a thornbush over me, and . . ." Mary gulped for breath, pushing her lank hair behind her ears. "And I saw *them*." She paused dramatically, hand outstretched.

"Who?" Lidda asked.

"A woman and the Devil riding a broomstick *right past my bedroom window*! I fell to the floor and began to pray to God to take this affliction from me, but their power came through the window and struck me—here!" She thumped her chest. "My legs began to writhe, my hair crawled, pins and needles pierced my flesh—oh, it was unbearable!" She clasped her hands together, a look almost of ecstasy on her face.

"How frightened you must have been!" Lidda stepped back a pace.

"Oh, I was, I almost lost my senses!" Mary trembled slightly as her mistress gave her a sharp look.

"I still think it odd that you did not come and wake us, Mary. I would like to have seen this, too, as would my husband."

"But he does not believe me," Mary whispered, rubbing her shoulders. As she headed for the kitchen, Lidda jumped up, saying, "Could I help wash the dishes, Mistress Proctor? I would hear more of this, and I see you know this tale already."

The woman nodded, lips pursed in disapproval, every angle of her body expressing disbelief and raw fury.

Lidda followed Mary into the room containing another big fireplace and a plank table, surface gleaming in the pale sun. A red pitcher stood in the middle, looking as if it waited for something marvelous to fill it—a yellow spring flower or a gathering of daisies. Lidda wished she had some right then to give her courage, for it was time to start confronting these lies, to become the kind of girl Lucian admired—strong, courageous, and full of spirit. Like Goody Bishop.

When the servant began washing dishes in a bowl, Lidda took up a linen cloth and dried them, setting them on the table for the next meal.

"Mary," she began, careful of her words. "I do not remember anyone else besides Tituba seeing women riding on a broom." Though she was beginning to lose track of who had seen what and when.

"Mayhap that is because I am not a girl like the others, Lidda Johnson. I am a grown woman of eighteen years, as you well know."

"I confess I am curious to know how the Devil appeared to you, Mary."

"Hairy, Lidda, just as Tituba said. All over hairy, with a long nose, and covered with black fur—horrible."

"Not—not beautiful in any way?" Lidda ventured.

"Beautiful? The Devil? Where are your wits, girl? There is nothing beautiful about evil! I know, I've seen it before, heard about it from my relatives who suffered attacks from the Indians. . . ." Her voice trailed off into a faint wisp. She pressed one hand to her side, taking a deep breath as if she herself had been the victim of an attack instead of her relatives.

With all of her senses alert, Lidda caught a faint trace of the scent of lies, and something else that emanated from Mary—something sour and bitter that she could not name. Was it envy? Gently she touched Mary on the shoulder. "I see this has been a trying time for you."

"Trying, Lidda! You know not—you with your secure household, with a papa and a mama to care for you, always enough to eat, never fearing where you might sleep the next night. . . . Mister Proctor beat me for telling what I saw. . . ." She trailed off. "But there is more. I vow the Devil was tall, dark, and wicked looking, like our enemies the Indians, with an evil heart inside."

"I am sorry for your trouble, Mary. Susannah is much concerned for you."

"Thank you, now I must be about my chores upstairs. We servant girls have no time to waste in idle chatter."

"But," Lidda called after, mustering her courage, "I do not believe the Devil is hairy or that he rides on a broomstick, asking women to write in his red book."

There, I said it. Are you not proud of me, Lucian?

There was no response; he seemed to have disappeared, which happened at times. Was he angry with her for asking questions? For chiding him about Charity?

At first Mary did not respond, except Lidda heard her footsteps stop overhead—a pause—then quick thumps as she ran back downstairs. Mary poked her head into the room and said, "How know you what the Devil looks like, Lidda Johnson? Have you seen him?"

"First, Mary, tell me if some of the other girls have told you what to say. Have they?"

Mary came closer to her, gave her a confused look, and shook her head.

"Ann Putnam did not give you a made-up story to use, to accuse people, where the girls would all say the same thing?"

Mary held out a hand and pushed Lidda's shoulder. "How can you say such things? This is the work of the Devil, Lidda Johnson. I see that!"

"The work of the Devil," Lidda muttered. She remembered the phrase that had burned into her mind when Papa read to them from the Bible, about the Devil being the father of lies. But now she *knew* who bore this name, and it was not Lucian.

"The father of lies is loose in our village, Mary, causing madness and confusion; making you girls accuse sick old women so they are jailed. The lies and the accusations—*that* is the only Devil abroad!"

"You lie," Mary said, "and I will tell the others—I do say, Lidda Johnson with your hateful accusations, that *you* may be the next one to be named!" The words fell like stones into the room, and both girls rocked back on their heels.

I will be accused next! Lidda thought. "Oh, Mary, 'tis not so, not at all—if you only knew"—she paused—"what I have gone through, what I know. . . ."

Mary came close, putting one hand on Lidda's. "Tell me, girl, what you know." Her voice was gentle, coaxing. "What have you gone through? You spoke as if you'd seen the Devil."

Oh, to tell someone! The relief it would be to share this disturbing, beautiful, seductive, and sometimes threatening presence! What would it feel like to unburden herself?

Lidda felt something stirring within, a swishing, a circling around—and faintly she heard an earlier threat from Lucian: *Do not ever tell or I will abandon you to your fate!* But now how was she to protect her family from disaster if Mary called her a witch?

"Lidda?" Mary breathed out. "Are you oppressed as well?"

"I sometimes fear, Mary"—her voice was a thread—"that I might be oppressed, too. I have seen such things . . . a voice, sometimes. . . ." Her words dropped at the end, like someone coming to the end of a song, spelling out relief, exhaustion, maybe even . . . hope.

Mary threw her arms around her. "Oh, Lidda, the Reverend called the Devil 'the fountain of malice,' and he can sound so sweet. I know! But there is help. We will find the cause of your oppression!"

She paused, looking at Lidda with avid eyes. "Who will you name, girl? Is it Martha Corey or Rebecca Nurse? Or someone else?"

A bitter wind chilled her insides, scouring her round and round until all that was left was a sense of whitened bones and a few fragments of tissue left clinging to them.

I warned you! The words snapped like a vicious whip, and . . . he was gone. Nothing was left, except the shell of herself.

"Here, Lidda, drink this." Mary held out a cup of cider but could not pour it into Lidda's mouth, prevented by the solid wall of teeth.

Mary set down the cup, patted Lidda awkwardly, and began to say the Lord's Prayer; but a roaring filled Lidda's ears, her sight disappeared, and she fell backward into darkness.

When Lidda awoke, she was laid next to the fire in the main room, with Mistress Proctor bending over her.

"Lidda, Lidda!" Her voice was high and frightened. "What happened?"

Lidda shook her head back and forth. Words had gone. He had taken them. They were sucked down inside and locked in a box out of sight. All she could do now was move her head from side to side and groan with emptiness.

"Oh, such a piteous sound!" Mary cried. "I do believe the Devil himself oppresses her! Tell us what you see, Lidda."

She whimpered. Just then, John Proctor strode into the room, bringing with him a brisk wind and an air of disapproval.

"Husband?" Mistress Proctor said. "Lidda has fallen ill in our house—we know not why—"

"It is the Devil himself that oppresses her!" cried Mary.

John lifted one blunt hand as if to strike his servant, but Mistress intervened. "No, not now, John, not now. It is one thing to strike your servant, but—look at the poor girl. Please, take Lidda home on your horse. She is ill and must be returned to her family."

Mister Proctor gave Lidda a searing look that went from the toes of her worn boots to her mussed linen cap. She felt flayed, exposed, but could say nothing to defend herself.

When he left to ready the horse, Mistress Proctor moved Lidda to a sitting position and wrapped her cloak about her. She rose and went to the cupboard in the corner, returning with a bag of dried lavender. "Here." She held it under Lidda's nose. "This will help you, child. Lavender is very soothing, as we all know."

Lidda inhaled the sweet scent and began to cry; it reminded her of her old life, the life before the heat, before Lucian, before the unbridled anger, before her thoughts became untethered and sailed off into the blue—the life she used to have where she picked sky berries with Charity, danced in the birch grove out of sight, and was innocent and free.

"Wait here. My husband will take you home." As if she could move, Lidda thought, as if her limbs would obey her even if she wished them to.

Mary continued to kneel by her, pressing her hands. Lidda wanted to tell her to stop, that no comfort came from her, but words stayed behind her teeth as if behind a shut gate.

John returned, pulled Lidda to her feet, threw her over his shoulder, and took her out to his horse. None too gently, he tossed her over the withers and swung up behind. Kicking the horse into a trot, he headed down the road toward home, and Lidda's head thumped against the horse's side again and again, as if John intended it, as if he meant to knock out of her all mention of the Devil and oppression.

21

SHE HAD BEEN SOMEWHERE, SHE WAS NOT sure where. There had been clouds whirling, bursts of light, and the growl of distant thunder like some vast beast approaching. Smells assaulted Lidda: first the sweetness of cut hay and meadow flowers, then the stench of cows kept in a barn all winter, followed by the odor of slaughter when a pig was cut open. Finally the raw, metallic smell of blood overpowered her.

In the stillness she heard a sound; after the thunder came a high, unearthly singing. Was it angels? Or something else? Later she heard trees rustling, fresh and gentle as a spring wind, but it did not last. Something huge and gleaming flew through the air, its wings beating hard, sending out a shrill whining. Lidda flinched and curled up tighter, trying to squeeze into herself. The creature intended to harm her, she knew. It would leap upon her, seize her in its claws, and rip her to pieces.

Then the sky turned bloodred, with flashes of gold and purple raindrops falling, falling, falling, and wherever they fell they burned. . . .

"Lidda, Lidda, wake up."

Who called her? Was it someone she loved or someone she did not?

"Lidda, please wake up." That sounded like Mama, a worried, scurrying voice like mice on a cold floor.

"Daughter, Lidda, please . . ." That must be Papa. He so seldom called her by her true name. What *was* her true name? Was it "girl," what Lucian called her? Once she thought he had called her Crisomou, golden one. She liked that name.

"Sister, please, sister . . ." That was Charity's voice. She struggled to open her eyelids, but they felt heavy as stones.

Someone took a small hand and patted her cheeks, murmuring, "Lidda, Lidda . . ."

That touch, that smell—she opened her eyes. It was Thomas, held close by Papa, patting her face and neck with light, warm touches. She held out her arms to her baby brother, seized him, and pressed him close. He snuggled into her neck, sighed, and promptly fell asleep.

"Thank God, praise God," Mama and Papa said together. They were both kneeling on the floor by Lidda, who found herself wrapped in a blanket near the fire.

"You were ill, sister," Susannah said in a happy voice. "Mister Proctor told us you had fallen onto the floor—a faint, he supposed!"

"Mmm . . . ." Lidda tested her voice. But there were no other sounds to follow; of course, if she was empty inside, how *could* she talk? It would be like the wind trying to find words.

"It seems to me, wife, that this is just like Zechariah in the Bible, who was struck dumb because he would not believe the angel's prophecy that Elizabeth, old as she was, would bear him a child."

Mama made a soft sound of assent.

"And it was not until the babe was born that he could finally open his mouth and say, 'His name is John.' A whole nine months without speaking!" Papa seemed awed by the Gospel story, and the rest of the family added little bits to the account, how no one had believed that a barren woman of Elizabeth's age could bear a

175

child. But she did, through God's mercy.

"But Lidda is not to bear a child!" Susannah said shrilly. "She could not; the shame would be too great . . . Lidda!" She knelt, peering intently into her sister's face, eyes prominent and staring.

Lidda restrained an impulse to punch a fist into Susannah's face. This was nothing like Elizabeth's story. She was mute for an entirely different reason—she was being punished, she knew.

Charity gently stroked her shoulder. "She is not with child, you silly sister. There must be some other reason why she cannot talk."

"But surely," Susannah said in an excited voice, "it is because my sister is oppressed. You saw how she was flopped over Mister Proctor's horse. He dumped her on the floor like a sack of grain, Papa! Who knows how the Devil works? If he can take on the shape of a good woman of the town, why cannot he take away my sister's voice?"

She began to walk about the room, waving her arms dramatically. "Perhaps he has taken Lidda's voice and is hiding it somewhere—in a . . ." She paused and pressed one finger to her top lip. "In his red book! He tried to get Lidda to sign his *book*, and when she didn't, he struck her mute! That is it, I am sure of it!" She whirled around at the end of the room. "And we know that the Devil has been at work in the Proctors' household, we know that!"

She crouched near Lidda's head, stroking her forehead softly. Lidda was startled. Never in all her life had Susannah touched her so tenderly.

Lidda waited for the curt voice within, but only heard . . . silence, empty as a hollow barrel. She did not even have the strength to wonder or feel sad right now. She was flattened, pressed out, like a piece of dough rolled thin by an energetic housewife.

"Speak to me, sister, tell us what you saw!" Susannah urged her, but Papa pulled her to her feet, speaking sternly.

"That is enough, Susannah! You can see your sister is exhausted. We know not what has happened, and I caution you to keep this tale to yourself."

"Yes, Papa," Susannah murmured, but Lidda did not think she could keep such a marvel to herself. In a matter of hours or less, she would tell what had happened to Mercy Lewis and Abigail Williams, and before they knew it, the whole village would be talking about poor, mute Lidda and embroidering the tale.

Lidda reached out a hand, clutching her sister's ankle. "Don . . . don . . ." was all she could get out of her rigid mouth. She lay back panting, tears rolling down her cheeks. More than anything, she did not want to be the object of anyone's pity or invasive concern. *Just leave me alone!* she wanted to scream, but words were gone.

"Shhh, let her sleep." Mama put a folded blanket under her daughter's head, tucked the other coverlet more firmly about her legs, then stood. "We do not know what happened. Mayhap tomorrow I can talk with Mistress Proctor, and Susannah, you can visit Mary Warren and find out what happened. But until then, I counsel . . ."—she stared hard at Susannah—"patience, silence, and kindness to your sister."

"Of course, Mama," Susannah said meekly. "Perhaps Lidda would like some hot tea with a dash of Papa's rum in it?"

"That is the first sensible suggestion you have made all day," Jacob said, sitting on the edge of the bench near Lidda.

Just staring at his honest, worn boots comforted her. They looked so ordinary, so everyday, like the life she had lost and sometimes yearned to have back. Would she ever dance under the birch trees again in the spring, or leap into the air, hoping to fly with the birds?

Did she hear the faint echo of a mocking laugh within? Lidda pressed her hands to her chest, praying that *he* had returned, but there was no other sound. And when Charity knelt by her, holding out a cup of tea with the heady scent of rum, Lidda struggled to sip it, coughing slightly. It burned all the way to her stomach. It burned the way her confession had to Mary Warren— her renegade, traitorous confession that had sent Lucian away and rendered her mute.

22

"HOW IS SHE?" SOMEONE WHISPERED, coming in the door, the sound a mix of concern, eagerness, and excitement. Lidda saw Mary Warren shedding her cloak, darting a sympathetic look that seemed as if she had practiced it.

Being mute had its advantages, Lidda decided. She wasn't expected to *do* anything, except sit and stare out the frost-covered window, or perhaps make some ugly gray knitted sock. That would be acceptable. But they could not know what it was like to be her—they never had known. That inside the empty shell of her body a bitter wind blew round and round, scouring her insides. Lucian was gone. Nothing could take his place.

"She's just the same" came Susannah's cheerful reply, glancing at Lidda.

She was certain that this was the first time Susannah

was proud to be her sister, instead of dismayed and disappointed. *Now* she had a sister who had been touched by a witch or the Devil; *now* she had a sister others wanted to interview, see, and perhaps even touch.

Ann Putnam sidled into the room just behind Mary Warren, pushing the hood off her hair with the same excited air. "How are you, Lidda?"

At least she addressed me personally, Lidda thought. She shook her head, touching her mouth gently to show that words were still hidden behind her lips.

"Ah." Ann gave a wise and knowing smile. "It can happen this way, I am sure, though *our* fits"—she swept her arm to include Mary—"are different, with more pricking and pinching and our limbs becoming stiff as winter boards. But witches can do *anything*!"

The words lay in the room, shimmering with a hidden energy. Lidda felt it, almost like the heat that had emanated from her middle during her bad times. But this was different; Ann's words felt feverish and contaminated, like a fresh pond a cow had peed into, making it unfit for anyone to drink from or scoop up water for household use—that happened in the summer; she had seen it many a time—something beautiful and innocent

181

turning into something ugly and poisoned. . . .

Charity touched her softly. "Sister?" bringing Lidda back to herself.

She pretended her thoughts were like chickens that needed to be gathered together. There, she chased one down, then another, forcing them into an imagined barn and slamming the door. Lidda summoned a bright smile, the smile of an ordinary girl who had just happened to be touched by the Devil. Or a witch.

Mary and Ann went closer to the fire, talking together. "But what *did* happen at your house, Mary? Did you see or hear anything? Was it Martha Corey's specter or Rebecca Nurse's?"

Lidda groaned and moved her hand.

"Oh, such a piteous sound, it wounds me," Mary exclaimed, turning to Lidda and patting her comfortingly. Lidda shook off her hand and moved farther away, giving her a barbed look. She did not want to be touched. Not by any one of them. *The murder girls,* Lucian had called them. And now they thought she was one of *them*!

Mama stood near Mary with a certain stiffness in her middle, as if there were fine whalebones going from her waist up to her chest. Her neck was flushed red, and

Lidda realized she was angry; she was going to do battle for her.

"Tell me all that you saw yesterday, Mary, and what you heard. Mister Johnson and I would like the truth of this matter."

At that moment, Papa and Jacob came in from outside, slamming the door and bringing a blast of fresh, clean air with them. Once their coats were hung on the pegs, they greeted the two visitors and waited for Mary's response.

"Well." Mary rubbed her head. "It is hard to remember exactly what happened, Mistress Johnson. Lidda came to offer sympathy for my travails. . . ." She paused, savoring the word and liking it. "Travails, and she came to help with the dishes, asking how I was afflicted. I told her!"

Mary waved her arms, her voice rising. "I told her about the moon like a great, evil eye outside the window . . ."

Lidda imagined the sharp words coming from Lucian: *The moon cannot be evil, you doltish girl!*

"And how I felt pricked and pinched, oppressed by some shade I could not see—not then—choked and pressed!" Mary put her hands to her throat, cradling it protectively.

Ann moved forward and touched her arm. "How frightening, how terrifying it all is!"

"Yes, I almost lost my wits!" Mary said loudly. "But after I described how hairy, dark, and wicked looking the Devil was, Lidda wanted to know if he was not beautiful."

The air vibrated with renewed energy as everyone in the room turned to look at Lidda. Carefully she kept her face blank, trying not to add to the hysteria.

"Then she wanted to know if you, Ann"—Mary pointed—"had not come to me with a plot to accuse the next person, telling me that a spirit of lies—the father of lies, she called it—was abroad in the village! But we know the truth, that the Devil has been at work in Salem!"

Susannah sat down on the bench, wiping her brow with the hem of her skirt. She breathed heavily, like someone who had run too fast. "The Devil at work," she murmured in a caressing voice.

"Then Lidda told me she thought she had been oppressed, too—something about seeing 'such things' and sometimes hearing 'a voice.'"

Again everyone turned to stare at Lidda, and she

tried to assume the expression of a girl who had been slightly wounded, but then healed, and also comforted by sharing this revelation. But she thought perhaps her mouth failed her and simply twisted at one end. No one must know that Mary had threatened her because Lidda accused her of lying. No one.

"Then . . ." Mary gestured at Lidda. "Her voice disappeared. She could not talk to me or answer or anything. She fainted, crashed right onto the floor!"

Susannah smiled, and Lidda thought she would have given much to have been there. What drama! What excitement!

Just then they heard a firm knock; at Papa's call to enter, the door swung wide and a heavily wrapped man lurched into the room. His eyelids were white with frost, and he brushed at them before slamming the door. With an audible sigh, he began the business of unwrapping the thick green scarf, revealing an older man with bushy eyebrows and a fierce expression.

"Doctor Griggs!" Papa said, welcoming him. "Come in and have a cup of warm cider."

"I thank you, but I have come to see your daughter, who I hear has been oppressed with muteness." He shook his head ponderously and came over to where

Lidda sat near the window.

It is like the tide on the beach, she thought, *people surging toward me, lapping at my feet, then the sea takes itself away again, back out beyond the horizon where only fish and flying birds and boats driving before a storm see it. . . . I wish I could be with the birds and the waves and the endless sky. . . .*

Doctor Griggs patted her knee paternally and asked, "Lidda, I understand your voice has disappeared. Is that so?"

"Mmmph," she replied, that being the best she could do and the only sound she was willing to make. She supposed she could scream if it came to that, if they kept crowding about her with their staring eyes and hot hands and horrible, sticky sympathy. . . .

Doctor Griggs continued. "We know that sometimes during their fits, a few of the girls choked on their voices and could not speak. But to stay mute is something new. The Devil works in mysterious ways."

All murmured and nodded, all except Jacob, Lidda noted. He kept his eyes trained on the doctor and did not seem impressed.

"Did you see the Devil, Lidda, or a witch?" Doctor

Griggs peered at her from under his bushy eyebrows. She shook her head.

"He did not speak to you or threaten you with silence if you failed to do his bidding?" Lidda shook her head again.

"He is in the room!" Ann declared in a shrill voice. "I can feel him—I see a yellow bird over against the wall there." She pointed with a shaking hand to a blank wall. "The Devil is telling us that we must sign his little red book with a black pen or we will all lose our voices!"

At that point, both Ann and Mary fell to the floor, elbows held out at an agonizing angle, mouths wide-open, eyes staring. Lidda thought she saw a spot of drool escaping from Ann's mouth.

Susannah looked as if she wished she could fall on the floor, too, but one stern look from Papa kept her pinned to her seat. Instead, she whirled her arms about, making odd noises like the wind.

"Stop that, sister!" Jacob said. "At once!"

"But I cannot, the Devil wills it," Susannah squeaked.

You will it, you silly girl. Stop it right now! Lidda wanted to shriek, but no sounds came forth.

"Enough, enough!" Mama commanded. "I will not

have people making my daughter worse—frightening her, stirring her up, and causing all of this confusion."

Papa jumped in. "There has been enough of fear. . . ." Flushed, he suddenly stopped what he was going to say, glancing sideways at Mary and Ann.

Ooh, that was not wise. Disagreeing is dangerous, I found out, Lidda thought.

But the sense of danger faded at the warmth flooding her body—warmth that her parents were beginning to see the malice of what was happening in the village, that they were protecting her.

Mary pulled herself up by the bench, dusting off her skirts. She held out a hand for Ann, who stood, a trifle unsteadily. They gave Papa and Mama mulish, defiant looks and murmured something about "unbelievers," but they did not stay, shrugging on their cloaks and hurrying out the door. Doctor Griggs followed soon after, wrapping up his face and plopping a thick felt hat on his head.

Lidda thought he looked much better with his face hidden, and she smiled briefly, surprised to see Jacob smiling in response.

Mama heaved a sigh of relief and took Thomas from

the cradle, holding him close. "There is too much . . ." She could not finish.

"Noise," Jacob finished for her. "And carrying on and talk of the Devil. I am tired of it!"

At last! I am tired of it, too, brother. Thank you for saying that!

"Well, dear one." Papa came and put one callused finger under Lidda's chin. "This is a great deal to endure, is it not? I like it not, not one bit!" He thrust his pipe into his mouth, lit the tobacco, and puffed angrily, white clouds sailing out in thick bursts to the ceiling.

I like it not either, Papa.

But the only one who disagreed stood and stared at them. Susannah exploded. "How can you say that? How *can* you? When you have seen how the Devil works in our village; when Mary and Ann actually *fell* to the floor and *saw* the little yellow bird, as they did when the men questioned Tituba. This tale is not over, I can see that; and our sister will have more to tell us when her voice finally returns."

Susannah turned to go upstairs, her stiff back expressing outrage and injured dignity.

"Well," Mama said, "I scarce know what to believe

anymore. What is true and what is not true?"

If ever there was a time when she needed Lucian, it was now, Lidda thought, putting a hand to her empty chest. *Truth and lies, girl*, he had told her early on, *and the wit to tell the difference.*

23

FOR THE FIRST TIME IN YEARS, LIDDA FELT accepted and loved. Her family circled around her as if she were a newborn, a precious gift from God. Papa made sure she had the best food at the table; Mama came up the stairs at night to cover her with another blanket, a luxury undreamed of. No one, except Susannah, referred to that visit from Mary and Ann, thinking it might upset her.

Even Susannah continued to show her a gentle affection, placing her warm hand over Lidda's at the table, offering her pieces of fresh bread. Only occasionally the words she was dying to ask rushed out, as they did several days later as light faded from the sky.

"Oh, Lidda, can you not talk now? Was the Devil hairy and dark? Did he hold out a black pen for you to write in his red book?" she asked, while Mama was out of the room and Papa and Jacob were tending stock in the barn.

"Stop it!" Charity said, coming over behind Susannah. "You know Mama said not to bother Lidda, and Papa agreed. She cannot talk. Leave her alone!"

Susannah stepped back a pace, surprised. "Well, I wished to know, Charity. It is best if we know how the Devil appears to us, then we can be prepared and ward off an attack." She went back to the fire, poking it vigorously, as if it were the fire's fault that she could not hear Lidda's amazing story.

Lidda wanted to tell her about the father of lies, how she thought there was a spirit of falsehood and cruelty abroad in the village—but not the Devil himself, for she did not even know if she believed in him, despite what Reverend Parris said. And, in truth, she did not believe that she had been oppressed—maybe "visited" was a better word. For months she had been home to something, *somebody*, but more than that she could not say. Only now Lucian was gone, she knew not where. He had vanished in the roar of an interior wind that day at the Proctors' house, and she was left, a hollow shell.

She wondered what her family thought about her

muteness; they did not speak of it, except Susannah, and Lidda had no idea if they thought she had been oppressed by the Devil or if it was some strange new development in the illness they had already seen in her: running out to the privy, flushing red, leaving the meetinghouse and dancing home. She had always been odd, and perhaps they thought this was just another part of her strangeness. That was a painful thought, and Lidda shivered, wrapping her arms around her middle.

"Lidda? Would you like some warm cider?" Charity asked. "I could put a little of Papa's rum in it, the way we did before."

Dear Charity always knew, Lidda thought. But taking Papa's rum from the cupboard? She didn't think he would be pleased with that, even if she was ill. "Ill." Was that the right word? "Stricken," perhaps, or "punished by absence," or "woeful" and "despairing." Those were all purple words, of a hue so dark they were almost black. She could feel the words circling about her head like heavy, sad birds. She did not think that hot cider or rum would help; but despite that, and because Charity gave her such a pleading, affectionate look, she nodded once. "Mmmph," she said, and

Charity smiled, seemingly happy to have even a fragment of sound from her sister.

First Charity filled a pottery mug with cider, then she went to the corner cupboard, bending over to retrieve a dark brown bottle stored on the bottom shelf. Carefully she poured a little into a spoon and tipped it into a mug. "There, sweetheart, this will be hot in a moment."

Susannah gasped and swung around from the fire, where she had been stirring the stew in the big iron pot. "Charity! Papa's rum!"

"Tish," Charity answered. "Lidda is ill and we must do all we can to make her well." She did not remind her that Susannah herself had suggested warm cider with rum the day Lidda was brought back—broken—from the Proctors' house.

Just then Papa and Jacob came into the room, knocking snow off their boots and shedding their coats. Fragments of chill, dark air fell onto the floor from the stiff cloth, Lidda saw. Bits of straw, too, and the smell of cows—rich, moist, and curiously satisfying. The warm-animal smell made her insides feel a little less hollow, less unsettled.

Charity took the iron poker from the wall beside the

fireplace and placed one end in the flames, kneeling down to tend it.

"What is this, child, what are you doing?" Papa asked, rubbing his hands briskly and coming closer to the fire.

"I am making mulled cider for our Lidda," she answered.

Papa nodded and said, "You are being a good and thoughtful sister."

In a bit, Charity took the rod out of the fire and thrust its reddened end into the mug of cider and rum. It hissed invitingly, and a fragrant smell rose. Lidda came closer, yearning for it and aching for that sound: the faint hiss, the faint sibilant sound that she had first heard from Lucian months ago.

"Here, drink this, you will feel better. Your voice will come back, I am sure of it." Charity handed Lidda the mug, and she sipped, giving a grateful sigh.

Soon Susannah served the stew into the bowls, and everyone sat at the table, eating in hungry silence, then talking about the news in the village.

"I still cannot believe that Ann Putnam accused Dorcas Good," Jacob said, scowling. "A four-year-old girl. How can that be? And to be in jail with her mother!"

Susannah snapped, "You do not know how the Devil works, brother. He can work through anyone of any age!"

Papa sighed, rubbing the top of his balding head, something he always did when worried or uncertain. "I cannot understand how the girls could have named Gospel Women from our church—Rebecca Nurse and Martha Corey. I know this happened a while back, but I am still not used to it."

Lidda thumped her hand on the table. Dear, elderly Rebecca Nurse, who often spoke kindly to Lidda after church? If only she could talk! She would scream and yell to protest this outrage.

But Mama said it for her. "If such women as these are accused, then none of us is safe." She gave a speaking glance to Susannah, who ducked her head, fiddling with her spoon.

Lidda could not help it. Tears poured out of her eyes, streaking down her cheeks. She could not prevent what was happening; she could not expose these girls as the liars they were because she was mute. She was helpless as a newborn child, silent as a whisper in the forest.

"What is it, dear?" Charity asked. "Would you like

to go to bed? Mistress Putnam had to rest under the covers after one of her attacks. I think you should, too."

Surprisingly, Lidda felt Jacob's hands under her arms, lifting her and helping her up the stairs as if she could not walk. She felt his labored breath against her neck, a kind of silent caring.

Once she was tucked into bed, Lidda watched him go, taking the lit candle with him. She made a sound of protest, waving her hand at the flame, and Jacob returned, setting the candle down on the chest by the bed.

"There, sister, you have been in darkness. Who needs this light more than you?" Carefully he took the edge of the coverlet and wiped the tears from Lidda's face, which only made her cry the more. He patted her hand awkwardly, turned, and left.

Perhaps someday my voice will come back. Perhaps Lucian will change his mind and return to me. Perhaps this madness in the village will end—somehow. If only I had something red and happy, like Goody Bishop's waistcoat, it would help. Perhaps . . . Lidda's fingers plucked at the coverlet, working it back and forth. *Perhaps I shall learn to live again, without Lucian.*

24

"SHOULD SHE COME TO THE EXAMINATION?"
Lidda heard Mama whisper to Papa in the far corner
of the room. Did they think her hearing had gone as
well? The words were clear as birds flying swiftly to
her ears.

"I know not, wife. It will be noisy—all of the
oppressed girls will fall to the floor, there will be
screams and shouts. Do we really want our own trou-
bled daughter to go through that? And it is a longer
walk now to Salem Town, where this examination will
be held."

Lidda jumped when Papa came over to the bench,
putting his hand on her shoulder. "Daughter?" he asked.
"Do you want to come to the examination of Mistress
Proctor and Goody Cloyce today?"

Lidda's eyes widened, and she shook her head

vehemently. "Nnnnn," she ground out. She was afraid that if she went to another lying congress of girls and villagers, she might do something dangerous, such as fling herself at Ann Putnam when she made her accusations.

"These are Gospel Women," Papa repeated, still baffled. "How could they be afflicting anyone?"

Susannah's voice was strident. "Their specters can do anything, Papa, I am sure of it! That is how the Devil works. And Goody Cloyce is Goody Nurse's sister—we know that witchcraft can be shared in families."

"You are very sure about a lot of things, daughter," Papa said reprovingly. "We shall see what we shall see in the meetinghouse."

Jacob said suddenly and surprisingly, "I wonder if Goody Cloyce is being accused because she slammed out of our meetinghouse that Sunday?"

Papa looked at him intently but did not answer. Only Susannah responded with "How could that possibly be, brother? What a foolish idea! Come, we will miss the beginning if we do not leave now."

Mama laid her warm shawl beside Lidda. "I am glad to leave Thomas with you. I do not think it a good place to bring a baby . . . somehow."

I do not either, Mama—witch girls, accusations, and pretend fits!

Lidda waved them off and was content to hold Thomas in her arms, walking back and forth across the room. Occasionally she put Thomas back in his cradle while she stoked the fire and stirred the baked beans. She imagined her family walking the five miles to Salem Town and sitting in the dark meetinghouse. She could see the table set up in front with the magistrates questioning Mistress Proctor and Goody Cloyce. All too vividly, her imagination pictured Ann Putnam, Abigail Williams, Mercy Lewis, and others falling onto the floor in their "fits" whenever the accused "witches" glanced their way. Papa had said that John Indian would be one of the accusers this time, which was odd.

The light was almost gone when the door opened and her family returned from the long walk. Mama looked exhausted, Papa had sweat on his brow despite the cold, Jacob looked disgusted and Charity saddened. Only Susannah seemed cheered by it all, somehow enlivened.

"Oh, you should have been there, sister!" she exclaimed. "The piteous moans of the girls! Their writhing on the floor! This time John Indian was one of the oppressed, and he shouted that the specters were choking him! Mary Walcott was there, too, with Mercy Lewis. Such . . ." Words ceased, and she waved her hands expressively.

"Such chaos!" Papa said.

"And pandemonium!" Jacob answered. "The shrieks, the yells, as if sheer noise were enough to accuse those two poor women of their guilt."

The entire family swiveled to gaze at Jacob.

"Just what are you saying, brother?" Susannah said, sitting heavily on a bench, not taking off her cloak. "Did not Abigail Williams tell about the witches' Sabbath she saw in the pasture? That red blood and red bread were being offered, but she refused?"

"I am saying that I am no longer sure of these accusations, sister, that is what I am saying." Jacob angrily pulled off his coat and slung it onto the peg on the wall. "How many times must we listen to these girls moan and shriek? How many times will we see our neighbors taken away to jail? Answer me that, sister!" He glared at her.

She glared back. "Clearly you do not believe the Devil is at work in Salem, brother. I am surprised at you, truly I am. How could there be all of these examinations unless the Devil really *were* at work?"

Lidda put out a hand and gently touched Jacob's sleeve, patting it again and again. Though she could not speak, her hands spoke for her, telling him she was proud of him, showing that she agreed with him.

He sat on the bench, pulling Lidda down beside him, smiling at her.

"Then how did our Lidda become mute, brother, I ask you that?" Susannah jumped to her feet and paced restlessly back and forth in front of the fireplace. "I ask you that?" she repeated.

"We do not know the answer to that, Susannah," Papa said in a tired voice. "Answers are not as easy as you seem to think they are. Perhaps Lidda has something wrong with her throat; perhaps it is a disease of some kind." He sent her a questioning look, and Lidda just shrugged her shoulders. She could not and would not tell her family the real reason for her muteness.

Jacob continued. "Just to be related to an accused witch seems to be enough to convict them. Is that fair? And was it fair the way Goody Nurse was sent off to jail?" He stared at Susannah. "I tell you, sister, I believe that old woman was hard of hearing. I remember her pausing before the magistrates' questions, and they thought her guilty because of her silence."

"Oh, husband, could that be?" Mama put a hand on Papa's arm. "Has justice been done? Did Goody Nurse's deafness send her to jail?"

"Nonsense!" Susannah exploded. "I can scarce believe what I am hearing in this house. Justice is being done, and this village is at war with the Devil, just as Reverend Parris has told us!"

Reverend Parris, Lidda thought bitterly. *With his arrogance, his certainty, and did he not beat Tituba to get her to confess?*

A weary look passed over Papa's face, and his hair seemed grayer and sparser. All that was happening was taking a toll on the family—the whole village, in fact. Lidda imagined Salem Village as some vast animal, sickening from a summer complaint—legs shriveling, hooves falling off, belly swelling with poison, and fever pricking the eyes and addling the brain.

When they sat at the table to eat, no one seemed to have much appetite, despite the hearty beans and fresh bread. They talked together, words coiling over the table like wisps of smoke. "Will be trials . . . once the new governor arrives . . . a commission will be appointed."

Jacob put his hand on Lidda's and said soothingly, "It will not last forever. Mayhap something will stop all of this madness." His voice was low, for her ears alone, so that Susannah could not hear and flare up again.

Mama lifted Thomas to nurse him. "How this village will survive is something I am beginning to doubt; who will plant the fields, if we're all in the meeting-house? Who will harvest the crops? Who will spin the yarn to make stockings and clothes?"

"Who, indeed, wife?" Papa said, trying to light his pipe and failing. "Who, indeed?"

Darkness and silence settled over the house, over the village where the wavering lights made no headway against the night. Once again, Lidda yearned for the presence of Lucian inside. He would make sense of this; he would have some fierce and penetrating comment to make about the proceedings in Salem. But would he be able to save them from the disaster of these trials, the lies and the suspicion? She was not sure that even a miracle from heaven could stop the madness, and she did not expect that to happen.

25

THE DAYS WENT BY, LIDDA DID NOT KNOW
how many, turning into weeks, for there were more than
a handful of Sundays when they went to meetinghouse
for services. Lidda kept herself rigid and silent on the
bench then, refusing to respond to anyone who spoke to
her, expressing sympathy for her muteness. Even when
Ann Putnam sat nearby one Sunday and put her hand
on her arm, Lidda shook it off fiercely.

"I am sorry for your oppression, Lidda," Ann said in
a faint voice, taken aback. "The Devil moves in mysterious ways." When she rose to join her family, Lidda gave
her a burning, derisive look. If only Lucian were here!

Madness, Lidda imagined him saying, *utter madness!*

At night, she lay quiet in the darkness, still hoping for
Lucian's voice to come back, hoping that if she turned
quickly enough to look at the clothes chest, he would be

sitting on top, asking, *Well, did you miss me, girl?*

But silence stayed, and what came to Lidda as she rested in bed were the names of the accused, like birds circling over her head.

If I just say their names often enough, they will not be forgotten, Lidda thought. *Even if I cannot speak them, I can remember them in my head.* So, like a child counting pebbles in the road, she held each name, dropping it into the dark: *Tituba, Goody Osborne, Goody Good, sweet Rebecca Nurse, respectable Martha Corey, little Dorcas Good*—Lidda paused and sucked in a breath after that name. Something that sounded like a cry bubbled up in her throat, but no one heard; no one else was awake. Then she continued: *now John Proctor, Elizabeth Proctor, even Mary Warren—her lies have come home to roost!— Goody Bishop is in jail, too—Abigail Hobbs, Deliverance Hobbs, and poor George Burroughs, from Maine.*

She thought that perhaps it was George Burroughs she had heard the girls plotting about that day sometime back in the Putnams' house, when they were whispering about specters. For now their former minister had been caught and brought back from Maine to be tried, all on the "evidence" of these girls, who claimed Burroughs's specter had oppressed them.

So the weeks went by, a round of food and silence, sleep and silence, as the wind freshened, birds returned, and Papa began to build houses again for those who needed them. Her family did not know what to do with her, except to lead her to a chair beside the window so she could look outside.

Occasionally Mama gave her some carrots or parsnips to chop for soup. One day she said, "Lidda, come here and try kneading bread. It will be good for you to do something, to feel useful again."

As she stood by the table, Lidda pushed out the dough, then pulled it back. It felt elastic, springy, reminding her of the time she'd seen Tituba kneading bread. If only she could ask if there were any news of her friend! Frantically she tried to summon words back into her mouth. "Br—" She tried, digging her fingers into the dough. "Br—" But that was all that would come out.

Mama looked up at her eagerly, hopeful that her long silence was at an end, but it was not to be. Lidda's hands trembled so that she could scarce hold on to the dough. She left the table and returned to her chair, trying not to listen to the sound of her mother's quiet sobbing.

Sometimes she sat with Thomas on her lap, glad of his warm weight, swaying from side to side and humming a song. In the old days, Mama would have chastised her for the lilting notes, but now she was so happy to have *any* sound from Lidda that she said nothing.

One sunny day as she sat by the window, Lidda saw sunshine on the path outside, the grass thick and green. People were going about their business. There was Mister Thomas Putnam striding down the street, his hair blowing back in the wind. There went Mistress Putnam, out for a walk with her daughter, Ann, as if nothing had happened, as if they were not at the center of the town's web of falsehoods and accusations.

A mangy brown dog picked its way along the road. He had a lean look, like the dog they had fed the witch cake to, made with Betty's and Abigail's urine. And what came of that? Nothing at all, only a terrifying rebuke from Reverend Parris and probably the suspicion that helped to put Tituba in jail.

Lidda tried to ask Charity about her friend, but only soft murmurings escaped her lips. *Haven't I been punished enough, Lucian? You've taken my voice and yourself away—is not that enough?*

Would she wake one day to his seductive voice asking, *Where is your courage, girl? I counted on you to expose these lies!*

How could she get him back? If she retracted what she had said to Mary Warren, if she told her family it was not true, would that bring him home? But she could not speak, and though Mary Warren had now been named as a witch, she could still accuse Lidda from jail. Lidda did not think she could lie, even for Lucian; what courage she needed to confront this madness in the village would have to come from her alone.

26

ONE MORNING LIDDA AWOKE FROM A vivid dream about Lucian. He was beautiful as ever— long black hair blowing in the breeze, light shining on his golden chest. Did he whisper, *Lidda, Lidda girl? When are you coming back to me?*

When am I coming back to you? *You are the one who left me!*

Had she mumbled in her sleep? For Susannah rose on one elbow, suddenly alert.

"What?" She pulled on Lidda's arm. "Did you *talk*, sister?"

Lidda shook her head. She knew that words were still locked away, but the dream gave her hope that she might once again regain her speech.

She got out of bed, dressed, and went downstairs, with Charity following close behind. After breakfast,

Lidda pointed to the door, then to Mama, lifting her chin in a question.

"Of course, daughter, go outside—sit in the sun and breathe in some fresh air. It is bound to help you." She smiled uncertainly and set Charity and Susannah to do the morning chores.

Lidda stepped lightly over the grass, swinging her arms and practicing small sounds. She paused under an apple tree covered with green leaves. When she looked up, hoping to see some other colors besides green— silver, purple, and gold—she realized that the intense colors she used to see had gone away. Even the dreaded heat seemed to have left for another country. She would gladly take back the heat and anger if it meant having Lucian again.

She heard the door opening, and Susannah ran toward her, followed by another figure. "Mary Warren has come to visit! She wishes to know how you are faring these days."

Faring? I fare ill, Mary Warren. I cannot speak, and my insides are barren like a woman who has lost a child.

Mary walked carefully over the grass, as if her gait were something she needed to practice. It had an occasional hitch to it. Lidda wondered if all that had happened to her had somehow unbalanced her.

Mary stopped beside Lidda, taking her hands in hers. "Lidda," she whispered, "I did mean to come before, I was so worried about you, but it has been a very confusing time at the Proctors' house. You may know that Mister Proctor and Mistress Proctor are in jail in Boston now? Then I was jailed for a time as well, until I began to—" She paused and sighed. "Accuse others again. It was the only way out of jail, Lidda."

Lidda's eyes widened, and she nodded vigorously. She felt a slight easing inside, a cracking like ice breaking up in spring. Truth. The power of it!

Mary stepped closer and whispered, "They would have hung Abigail Hobbs, you know, except she confessed to being a witch and then made accusations too." Mary sighed. "It has all been so confusing, I must tell you—and you I can tell because you cannot speak now, and is that not an odd thing to happen to you? Did the Devil suck away your words, Lidda?" She peered at her, as if by looking hard enough she could divine where they had gone. "Oh, Lidda, I must tell someone or lose my senses, though at times I think I have already lost them!" Mary pressed her hand on

212

Lidda's arm. It felt warm, sweaty, and animal.

Lidda made a questioning sound and raised her chin.

"At first I was so caught up in the accusations, Lidda. Truly, it was like a heady brew from a tavern—my senses were all in a whirl. Ann Putnam made the first accusations, but then I also named my master and mistress. Who else could have caused that devilish tingling on the night of the full moon?"

Lidda shook her head and made a disapproving sound.

"You cannot know how dreadful it is to be in jail, Lidda. I would rather lose my voice than be imprisoned again."

Lidda stared at her, wondering where this was going. Mary was behaving like a child who had something to confess, who had gotten her best skirt wet in the stream behind the barn, or who had dropped a silver spoon down the well.

"I was not the only one to name witches!" she said shrilly. "There was Ann, too, and Elizabeth, Mercy, and Mary Walcott. It was like a fever!"

Lidda felt the heat from Mary's hand searing her arm, and she tried to shake it off; but Mary simply pressed closer.

"Then you confessed to being oppressed when you

visited us—but I will tell you, Lidda, that sometimes I think I lied. Some of my words were not God's truth."

Lidda put one hand to her stomach. The feeling of ice breaking up inside increased, gathering force and speed.

"I got caught up in the witch-fever, and I do not know what to do!" Mary wrung her hands together. "I wish you could tell me what to do. You were not lying— I know it. I saw how you writhed on the floor—not the way Ann Putnam does in the meetinghouse."

She tells the truth—the truth!

Something rose from within, and suddenly, there was a roaring in her ears, a sense of distant waters rushing over her. Her eyes spun backward, turning everything black. But the world beneath her eyelids was not dark— it was filled with bright lights and floating orbs. Voices she could almost name gathered there, clustered around the floating balls of light.

When Lidda came to, she was on the grass, with Mary bent over her, patting her face and crying. Her tears fell on Lidda's eyes, face, and mouth, washing them clean.

Words hurtled toward her, one by one, winging

their way, filling her mouth with their unaccustomed shapes and sounds. Lidda gave a great cry and opened her mouth.

"Oh, Mary!" She seized her hands. "You must tell the truth, girl, it is the only way out of this horror. Tell them that you did not know what you said!"

"Lidda . . ." Mary faltered and tried to stand. "You can talk. . . . I—I would not have told you this had I known you could talk . . . again. Susannah said your mouth was stopped up, like a summer well. That she doubted you would ever talk again. You would have to live with your mama and papa until they died, a useless old woman, silent as the grave." Mary plucked at her lip.

That was what her sister thought of her. All this time, Lidda had thought her older sister was compassionate, that the old bitterness between them had disappeared. Nothing had truly changed, then.

And now? She leaped to her feet, dancing from side to side. "Oh, Mary, I am so grateful to you! You have opened my mouth and released my tongue by telling the truth!"

Mary stood, turned quickly, and ran around the side of the house. Lidda thought she was sobbing, or perhaps gasping for breath. She did not care. She felt she had been living under the covers on an old and musty bed, and suddenly the blankets had been thrown off, and she stood in the sunlight with spring all around.

Lidda put one foot into the pool of light, took it out, then put it back in. Her foot—even in this old boot—looked beloved, well known. She danced lightly around the yellow circle, singing for the first time in months.

She could talk! And even if the magical presence of Lucian had gone, she almost felt herself again. Looking up into the boughs of the apple tree, Lidda spied the bright red bird with a tufted crest. He opened his mouth to sing, and Lidda stood beneath, taking his sweet notes into her mouth and swallowing them down.

27

EXCITEMENT BLEW THROUGH THE HOUSE.
Lidda could almost taste its sharp scent. The first trial
of the accused witches would take place tomorrow, June
second, Jacob informed them after supper, laying down
his clay pipe. A soft wind blew through the open door as
light thinned over the houses.

"It will be held in Salem Town," Papa declared.
"They expect a crowd of people from all the neighbor-
ing towns, and that is where the Court of Oyer and
Terminer will be gathered."

"Thank God, at last," Mama exclaimed. "Mayhap
there will be an end to this madness! At least Lidda can
talk again, and that is a sign of hope for the future!"

Madness, Lidda thought, remembering Lucian's
mocking voice. *They know nothing of it. This is witch-
fever, vengeance, and cruelty.*

"It is not hopeful, however," said Papa, scrubbing the top of his head, "to think of how many from our village and nearby towns are in jail."

"Where they should be!" Susannah declared.

"Why should they be in jail?" Lidda asked.

"Where else could they be?" Susannah replied. "They have to be locked away so they cannot harm any more children in the village!"

Papa shook his head, and Mama said nothing in reply either. Jacob rubbed his nose thoughtfully and said, "Do we even know what truly happened, sister? I have been watching Ann Putnam and the other girls at the examinations, and it seems too neat, too quick the way they fall on the floor at the same time, mimicking the same motions as the accused."

Susannah gasped. "But . . . witches . . . hurt . . . children!"

Lidda gave her brother a brilliant smile. He saw! "Oh, brother, I am glad to hear you say that."

"Still," Papa added, "we must be careful in what we say. The accusations follow thick and fast on anyone who protests these proceedings. Look at what happened to John Proctor!"

Mama encircled Thomas with her arms. "I wish it were over."

"So do I," Lidda answered as Charity agreed at the same time. Their perceptions, their refusal to believe ill of the accused, heartened Lidda and gave her courage for what was to come.

They went to bed early, while the sky was yet light, and it was a long time before Lidda closed her eyes and finally slept, clutching her hands together as if somehow that would give her strength for tomorrow. For tomorrow—tomorrow—it must be. She must speak out at last.

The next morning, the day of the trial, they rose early and ate cold porridge in the dawn before setting off on the long walk to the meetinghouse in Salem Town.

"Governor Phips assembled this court," Papa said, straightening his good waistcoat and moving toward the door. "I pray that we shall see justice done."

Jacob snorted. "We shall see about that, Papa. There is no guarantee."

This time Lidda took her brother's arm and walked beside him out into the bright light of morning. She blinked. A crowd of neighbors dressed in their finest were already on the road, hurrying toward Salem Town. Reverend Parris strode by, accompanied by his wife, thin as a wraith and gray about the lips. Betty was not with them—Lidda knew she had been sent away in March to stay with friends—but Abigail trotted beside them, an eager expression on her face.

Abigail Williams! Lidda could imagine Lucian's voice within. *That liar, one of the worst, except for Ann Putnam, who has brought down more people than anyone else. She and her mother and their fits!*

As people nodded and smiled at one another, Lidda found that her mouth didn't work properly. She did not know how to smile at those she did not love. The edges would not tip up anymore but stayed in a flat line. Was it the absence of Lucian that did this, or was it the false-hoods in the village that had thinned her mouth?

She knew what lay ahead. Would she be able to pro-test without Lucian to encourage her? The women would be brought out. The judges, all of them men, would ask, "Why have you hurt these children?" The witch girls would fall into fits on the floor, grimacing, howling, and claiming to be pinched and bitten. And now a new thing had happened: If an afflicted girl touched an accused witch, her fits would stop, and she would become calm.

It was a clear sign of guilt. Then, Lidda knew, one of the supposed witches would be taken to a place of hanging, her life choked out by the rope, her spirit flying into the bright air, but not before her tongue protruded and her eyeballs popped out and her bowels—what *did* happen to the bowels?

"Lidda! Are you all right?" Jacob shook her arm gently. "You seem flushed, overheated, sister."

Lidda sucked in a breath and tried to calm herself. She remembered long ago at the supper table when the heat had surged over her head, how Lucian had told her to imagine a cold place of retreat. She did that right now, holding inside the picture of Papa's icy woods with a chill wind blowing.

She was able to walk more swiftly then and to be calmer, even though it seemed they walked forever. Jacob gave her an encouraging smile when they finally reached the meetinghouse in Salem Town, joining the people clustered outside the doors. There were so many of them that it took a long time to file up the stairs and take their seats on the hard benches within; the light was faint and dim through the small windows.

So dark, Lidda thought. *Not the kind of darkness Lucian liked. Come back*, she whispered. *I promise not to chide you for criticizing Charity. I need you here today.*

"What did you say, sister?" Jacob said, steering her toward a narrow wooden bench.

Lidda stared at his round, honest face, with the dark beard edging his chin. He was proud of that and had been growing it all winter. She looked over at her family arrayed on the benches, all shoulder to shoulder in the press of the crowd—so many people, so many whose faces she did not know. They all looked like people with everyday lives, not the sort of people who would have a presence within. *Like me.*

There was Mama, appearing worn, arms holding Thomas, who slept with his head on her shoulder. Papa shifted on his seat, trying to get comfortable. Susannah did not seem to notice the hardness beneath; she leaned forward, elbows on knees, staring at the front of the room, where a long table had been set up. Sitting around it were seven men—the judges, all with somber faces.

Lidda tried to breathe and felt panicky. Already it was airless and strong smelling in the packed room. Charity touched her briefly.

"All right, Lidda?"

"Hush!" Susannah scolded them, sitting up. Her eyes gleamed with anticipation; and with sharp motions, she tugged at her bodice, smoothing imaginary wrinkles, as if she had to be clean and neat in this atmosphere of contamination.

There was a sudden flutter of movement around the room as the accused were brought in: respectable old Rebecca Nurse, who tottered as they led her to a chair. Goody Nurse's hair was disheveled and wispy, her dress wrinkled, as if she had been kept in a small jail cell. Beside her sat Deliverance Hobbs, a robust, red-faced woman; and next to her was Goody Bishop, looking defiant and stubborn, dressed soberly in black this time, with her gray hair pulled back. Lidda thought the man could have been gentler with Goody Bishop as he led her to the chair; the knuckles of his hands were white as they pressed on her arms.

"I am not going anywhere," Lidda heard her say. There was no hint of the old defiance in her voice.

"Goody Bishop," one of the judges intoned as he stood. "You are accused of being a witch, and though you confessed in your examination earlier that you did not know what a witch was, we have seen that the Devil can work through his minions in clever and insidious ways. You can be a witch and claim not to know it."

The crowd rustled with satisfaction; here was a good

223

beginning to the first trial. Things would be set out clearly this time.

He is weaving a net with words to catch her, Lidda thought.

"Why do you hurt these children?" the examiner said, repeating the question they always asked.

Goody Bishop replied, "I do not hurt any children. I scorn to harm them." She tilted her head to one side, looking confused.

Abigail Williams tilted her head to one side, too, as did Ann Putnam and several other girls.

"You see how you affect these poor children, Goody Bishop!" thundered the man.

"I do nothing to them, sir." Goody wrung her hands, and the girls all wrung their hands at the same time.

Mercy Lewis cried out, "Oh, Goody Bishop, did you not come to our house last night?"

Goody Bishop shook her head, and the girls followed. In unison, they fell to the floor and began to writhe about, shouting and calling, "Stop torturing us, Goody Bishop, stop it!" Their cries flew to the rafters of the wooden ceiling.

Lidda stared at Goody Bishop, feeling the words pelting against her own skin just as they must against the accused woman. She hunched her shoulders, gripping her hands tightly together.

Trying to ignore the raucous noise, the examiner continued, reading from a page held in his left hand. "Goody Bishop, we have heard the testimony of your minister, Reverend Hale, that after your neighbor Goody Trask complained of the late-night noise in your tavern, she fell into a distracted state of mind. Some months later, she killed herself."

Goody Bishop shook her head and said, "I did not cause her death."

The girls cried out again, and their arms froze into positions of pain.

Lidda felt the air in the room closing in on her, and she began to breathe in sharp, shallow pants.

"We have heard before that Richard Conan said you and three other witches appeared at night to torment him in his room. He had to sleep with a sword, and you witches tried to take it away!"

The noise of the afflicted ones subsided for a moment, as if they were concentrating on the testimony.

"Your neighbor's servant, John Lauder, told us how you appeared to him as a specter and choked him in his bedroom. This happened after he told you to keep your chickens out of his orchard."

The woman was silent, a bitter and resentful look on her face. Lidda was certain that she knew her fate and knew she was powerless to prevent it.

"And"—the man waved his hand dramatically—"John also saw the Devil with a monkey's body, cock's claws, and a man's face. He hit at it, but there was no firm body."

Lucian would mock those words, Lidda knew. Perhaps they were all drunk on strong wine?

"I know not what my neighbor did, nor what dreams he had," Goody Bishop protested.

"Then," the examiner continued relentlessly, "there is the testimony of John and Rebecca Bly, who bought a sow from you, which suffered fits after they delayed payment to you. They also found poppets in the old cellar of your former husband's house. We know that poppets are used in witchcraft to cast harmful spells!"

Poppets, a poppet, a locket, a song a lover would sing to his beloved. I bought my love a poppet . . . how could anything so harmless be so wicked? Lidda pressed her hands to her hot cheeks.

The people in the large room rustled and moved on

the benches; a few women sighed and moaned.

"I know nothing of this! I made no poppets!" Goody Bishop protested.

"Do you deny harming Samuel Shattuck's boy so that he fell, bruised himself, and had fits?"

Goody Bishop shook her head, and the girls on the floor writhed and shook their heads at the same time.

Lidda shook her head with them, trying to cast off the heat that was rising from her stomach, up her throat, her face, then surging over the top of her head. And with it came a blinding anger. Her fingers curved into claws. This must be stopped!

"William Stacy also accused you of killing his little girl, Priscilla, and appearing at the foot of his bed as a specter." The man rattled the written page in a threatening manner, glaring at Goody Bishop.

With the heat slamming through her body, Lidda jumped to her feet. "Stop, stop it! How can Goody Bishop defend herself? These accusations—the people afflicted—how—" She stuttered for a moment, the words pressing against her lips. Susannah grabbed hold of her skirt and tried to drag her down, but Lidda pulled away, pushing the words out of her mouth.

"How could one person's spirit afflict so many? It makes no sense! And look at those girls writhing on the floor. It is always the same. Once at Ann Putnam's house, I overheard the girls plotting details of the next accusation!"

"Sit down, sit down and be quiet, girl!" The examiner pointed at her.

"I will not sit down and be quiet. I WILL speak! Mary Warren confessed to me that she lied!"

Someone called out, "But she recanted that later."

"Yes," Lidda shouted, "because she knew she would be condemned as a witch if she did not! You are sending these women to their deaths—poor old Rebecca Nurse, who never hurt anyone—and Goody Bishop, who wears red and runs a tavern. Is that reason to condemn her?"

The room fell silent for a moment; Thomas stirred and uttered a small cry. What had she done? Lidda suddenly felt as if she were standing on a small island in the midst of a raging river. Faces turned toward her, questioning, avid faces.

Ann Putnam cried out from the floor, "Lidda Johnson, you are lying. We know these to be witches!"

"I do not lie! It is you who lie, and may your words

come back to choke you in the end!" Strength surged through her; and Lidda dashed from the room, hurtled down the stairs, and raced into the fresh air, taking deep gulps.

Voices and shouts from inside rose and swelled through the open door, the sounds cruel as a cat's claws raking across her skin.

They will come for me . . . come . . . later they will . . . and catch me like a wild animal in the woods . . . the woods . . . and they will carry me to the tree . . . the tree . . . and string me up beside Goody Bishop . . . string me up . . .

Feet pounding over the packed earth of the road, Lidda knew she would have to flee, but where? Was there any place on this earth that would be safe?

28

THE VILLAGE WAS EMPTY WHEN LIDDA raced down the road, up the stone steps to her kitchen. Inside, the fire still smoldered in the fireplace, a reminder of ordinary life, of porridge eaten with her family, of conversations around the table, all that she had ever known.

Holding a hand to her side, Lidda sucked in a breath. It had taken time to run the distance home, and she was already tired. She would need food. There was a dish towel hanging over Papa's chair, which she snatched up, throwing some bread inside, cheese, and a few wrinkled apples from the bowl. It would be enough to keep her from starving on the road, wherever she was going. *Going, I am going . . . at last, at last.*

Lidda raced upstairs, opened their clothing chest, and took out her winter cloak, a change of shift, and her ordinary skirt and bodice, bundling them together inside her gray cloak. *Someday I shall have a red cloak . . . red as my cheeks, as Thomas's nose . . . a sweet, bright red . . . like Goody Bishop's waistcoat.*

Lidda paused in her haste. Even now, Goody Bishop was awaiting her sentence, along with Rebecca Nurse and the others. Would she bow her head at the end? Lift it up and cry out defiance? She thought Goody might.

Do not slow down. . . . Do not . . . Keep hurrying before they return.

Lidda whirled about the room, saying good-bye to everything in it: Charity's trundle bed (*Good-bye, Charity, dearest sister, good-bye!*); the clothing chest where she had first seen Lucian sitting, months ago; the window that overlooked the meadow (*Good-bye, good-bye*).

Running downstairs, Lidda paused for breath beside Thomas's cradle, dear Thomas, with his eyes like blackberries and his lusty yells. *I will miss you most of all . . . how my songs always made you sleep. . . .*

Out the door. Out! She could not let herself waste time mourning. Lidda hesitated on the bottom step. Where? If she went into the woods, they could not find her. She could sleep wrapped up in her cloak at night and make her way to . . . Boston. She slapped one hand against her skirt. That was it! Boston! It was only a few days' journey away, if she walked fast, and there she could disappear into the crowds like a fish slipping beneath a rock. No one would find her there; no one need know about the heat that raced over her head, about Lucian who used to live inside.

Hurrying across the meadow behind their house, Lidda reached the edge of their woods. Shadows dappled the ground beneath, and she drew in a breath of relief as she ran under the trees. Turning, she looked back at the house where she had spent all of her days.

Will I miss them?

But who was that running toward her across the field, waving his hat and shouting, "Lidda, Lidda, wait!"

It was Jacob! He ran up to her, bending over and taking deep breaths. "Sister, you do run fast . . . wait . . . Papa gave me this to give to you." Jacob thrust one hand into his pocket and brought out a small leather purse, giving it to Lidda, who tucked it into her pocket under her skirt. "Papa said you must leave the village, else they will hang you too." He clasped her in a tight hug. "You were very brave, sister.

"Take the money, go where you must, and when you find a place, try and send us a letter that you are safe. Mama and Papa will want to know that—and Charity—and I," he said, with a slight quaver in his voice.

"Oh, Jacob, Jacob!" All this time she feared she was alone, and now it seemed that was not so. What a cruel situation. But she had to leave, had no choice now, and in truth, she did not wish to stay any longer in this place of vile and poisonous people.

"I must leave—now, before they come for me. Goodbye, Jacob, good-bye to everyone!" She turned once, waved, and headed for the tall pines in the woods. Over in the corner, a brown cow eyed her and gave a loud bellow. She was glad it was not a bull. Then she was brushing under the pine branches, and the sweet scent spilled around her like summer rain.

Swiftly she headed deeper into the cool woods. She wished Lucian were with her, to fill up the space inside. She tested the inside of her head, the place that she imagined was like a small, windowless room. When Lucian had lived within, sometimes her head was hot and filled with panic; but at other times a breeze seemed to blow through, bringing raucous singing, a dash of courage, and mocking comments on the villagers. The voice had kept her company all the time, even when she did not want it.

She had thought she would get used to his absence—it had been well over two months now—but she was not used to it. Her head felt like a bare, swept room. He had promised to be her only friend and companion, but it was an empty promise.

Once Lucian told her he admired her spirit; would he not be proud of her, the way she stood up and accused the lying girls in front of everyone at the meetinghouse? No one else had done so!

From a tree overhead, a vivid red bird took flight, seeming to carry all of her desire for a wild and free life, full of color and vibrancy, a life free of this stifling village. Wind rustled the leaves, sending them spinning in the clear light. Rimming the edge of each green leaf was a radiance, as if light itself were flowing out of every leaf.

Light. Everywhere. She held up one hand, turning it slowly back and forth. Her fingers blazed with it. Even the sky contained it—arcs of brilliant color—red, purple, and gold, sliding into drops like bright rain.

Suddenly, in the room that was her mind, Lidda sensed windows being thrown open, wind rushing in, and light streaming. She laughed, raising her arms to the sky like someone waking from a deep sleep.

Peering up at the sun through the leaves, Lidda headed southeast toward the coast to Boston. Her heart pounded with a strange excitement. This was her life now, not someone else's, not controlled by the rules of the village. She could be who she was, with no one to criticize her. And she would make certain to skirt around Salem Town, where she might be recognized.

She felt the comforting weight of the purse within her skirt pocket; it would help her find a place to lodge and would buy her food while she searched for a position in some household. Even if she was running toward freedom, it was good to carry a bit of safety with her. And she would take with her forever the warmth of Jacob's last hug.

Laughing and whirling her arms, Lidda passed under an enormous green pine, its branches swaying gently in the breeze. She stopped to listen. There—on the wind. She cocked her head, listening harder—she heard a faint laugh—mocking and entirely known. *Girl . . .*, the wind whispered. Again. *Girl . . . did you miss me?*

And louder now, more clearly, that decisive voice. *Girl, I have been waiting for you. . . . You showed them. You were brave. . . .*

She fell to her knees on the ground, ready for him to come home again, to fill all the interstices of her body, to fill the empty crevice in her middle. As the leaves swung from side to side in the breeze, she caught glimpses of a face—a fall of black hair, a disembodied smile, and two silver eyes smiling at her, alight with knowledge.

ABOUT BIPOLAR DISORDER

At the time of the Salem witch trials, no one knew about bipolar disorder, a mental illness. It almost certainly existed in past ages; some think that people who reported visions and voices may have had bipolar disorder. In our age it is a illness that is recognized and is more frequently diagnosed than ever before. Scientists are not entirely sure of its causes, although genetics play a large part; bipolar disorder tends to be passed down among families. Because countries where people eat a good amount of fish have lower rates of this illness (England and some Nordic countries), it is possible that there is a nutritional component as well.

Bipolar disorder is marked by strong mood swings—from depression to a kind of wild excitement called mania. The very word "bipolar" means "two poles." During a manic episode, a person might drive his car too fast; her thoughts can race (like Lidda's) and she may speak rapidly. In this state, a person might run out and spend thousands of dollars on clothes at a store or lose control in other ways. Sometimes during the manic phase of this illness, a person might see people who are not there or hear voices inside his head; we call these hallucinations. Seeing light rimming objects and colored rain can also be a part of the manic phase.

During a depressive episode—which often follows a manic phase—someone with bipolar disorder might find it impossible to get out of bed, continue with everyday life, or interact with people. Suicidal thoughts can be part of this depression. Visual and auditory hallucinations can be present in both phases of this illness, and can sometimes have a very dark and demonic quality.

Bipolar disorder may develop during childhood, but frequently it appears during puberty or in late adolescence. In this day and age, it can often be managed successfully through a combination of medications, changes in behavior, therapy, good nutrition, and healthy living. But at the time of the Salem witch trials, no one would have known what Lidda was suffering from, and she herself did not know.

You will see in the book that Lidda's "episodes" do not follow any regular pattern. Her hallucinations can appear at any time, and they can disappear for a long interval. So a person with bipolar disorder can seem relatively healthy and stable for a period and then become destabilized.

As for Lucian . . . was he real or was he a hallucination, part of what we call the psychotic element of bipolar disorder? Was Lidda mad, or was she saner than the villagers? You decide.

WHAT IS TRUE AND
WHAT IS NOT TRUE

The whole historical understanding of the Salem witch trials has changed over the years. Many explanations have been put forward for the bizarre behavior of the mostly adolescent girls, as well as the young women who also were accusers. One scholar theorized that ergot mold in the Puritans' bread caused hallucinations. Another scholar proposed that the bite of mosquitoes had given people encephalitis, a sort of brain fever, producing the odd actions of the afflicted girls. But more solid historical research has put forward a combination of reasons for this "witch-fever," as I like to call it:

• A lack of constructive ways for resolving disputes in the village (pointed out by Paul Boyer and Stephen Nissenbaum in their book, *Salem Possessed: The Social Origins of Witchcraft*); the village had a history of contentious dealings with their pastors.

• Property disputes among the villagers, particularly

between the Putnams (whose land holdings were decreasing along with their wealth) and other villagers, including the powerful Porter family (also pointed out in Boyer and Nissenbaum's book).

• Tension and fear caused by the border wars with Native Americans as close as seventy miles away; some of the young women who were accusers were survivors of these border wars and may have suffered from post-traumatic stress disorder (Mary Beth Norton forwards this view in *In the Devil's Snare: The Salem Witchcraft Crisis of 1692*).

• The influence of the Reverend Parris, an ego-tistical, vain man with a strong sense of his own importance, who preached frequently about the influence of the devil.

• The fact that girls were lowest on the social totem pole in Puritan society, with little power, visibility, or voice; the accusations and trials gave them undreamed-of power, and they were listened to as never before.

• The adult men in the village chose to believe in and emphasize the girls' reports of being "afflicted" and look toward a legal solution—not all villages responded in the same way as Salem did regarding charges of witchcraft (Norton).

• One girl allegedly told a Salem man that "she did it for sport; they must have some sport" (Boyer and Nissenbaum, page 9). If this is true, we could use the word "wicked" to describe the girls' accusations and the destruction of innocent lives.

These are some of the factors at play during this vivid and disquieting period in history. As a fiction writer I have used actual historical persons in this novel; only Lidda and her family are invented. I have also taken the liberty of changing some of the time line of events during this period. There is disagreement among scholars about Bridget Bishop and whether she might have been confused with another Bishop—Elizabeth, who may also have been a tavern keeper. Bridget Bishop (the first "witch" executed, in June 1692) lived in Beverly and had apparently never seen the girls in Salem Village who accused her. But Nathaniel Saltonstall himself—one of the judges in the Court of Oyer and Terminer (French for "to hear and determine," Norton, page 169), which pronounced legal sentences on the "witches"—said that Bridget was being condemned for wearing red, for allowing shuffleboard to be played in her tavern, and for being argumentative.

When Mary Warren came to talk with Lidda, confessing that she may have lied, Mary was actually still in jail and wasn't released until June. I have moved back her release a few weeks for plotting purposes. Also, Mistress Putnam's first "fit" occurs earlier in my book than in actual history.

Current research tells us that Tituba, the West Indian slave, never actually conducted fortune-telling gatherings at Reverend Parris's house. It is true that Tituba played a crucial role in the widening and deepening of the witch-fever by accusing other women of wanting to harm the children, namely Goody Good and Goody Osborne. Some historians wonder what would have happened had Tituba simply kept her own counsel and not confessed to being a witch. Perhaps it would have all died out. Ironically, although Tituba confessed to being a witch, she was not released from the Boston jail until a year later, and was sold as a slave to another man.

Other than that, the events in this fictional account follow the basic time line of the initial afflictions of the girls, their first accusations, the examinations of the "witches," and the first trial. Some of the dialogue used in chapters 19 and 27 comes from historical transcripts.

It is a curious period in history, and one that is difficult to read about. Based on the close similarities between various girls' accounts, I believe there was a conspiracy among the girls to share details of their afflictions and to decide whom to accuse next. (Norton, page 307, proposes that the accusations of George Burroughs resulted from the girls' collusion.)

I also believe that events got away from them, and that the attention given the girls and the power thus gained were a heady brew that they could not put down. In other witch trials in the colonies, once the "witches" were put behind bars, the accusations died out. But not in Salem. Events and the accusations did not stop until Governor Phips disbanded the Court of Oyer and Terminer in the fall of 1692, called a halt to all further trials, and freed the remaining people jailed in Boston. But this did not happen until after one hundred fifty men and women had been accused and thrown in jail (Boyer and Nissenbaum, pages 30–31); nineteen men and women had been hanged; one elderly man, Giles Corey, had been pressed to death by stones; several people had died in jail; two dogs were hanged for associating with witches; and one little girl, Dorcas Good, went mad while confined in irons with her mother in jail.

In the years after the trials ceased, several people came forward to confess and repent, among them Ann Putnam Jr. (one of the foremost accusers), who said she was confused and in error. Reparations were made to the families who had lost members to the executions, and a memorial was built; but oddly enough, it wasn't until the mid-1990s that the Massachusetts state legislature formally absolved the last Salem "witch" of all wrongdoing.

Truly, it was a devilish, grim, and compelling time in United States history; and it reminds us of how easy it is to be swayed by events, how easy it is to judge and condemn others, and how easy it is to be mortally wrong.

SOURCES FOR
FURTHER READING

Boyer, Paul, and Stephen Nissenbaum. *Salem Possessed: The Social Origins of Witchcraft*. Cambridge: Harvard University Press, 1974.

Demos, John. *The Enemy Within: 2,000 Years of Witch-Hunting in the Western World*. New York: Viking, 2008.

Hawke, David Freeman. *Everyday Life in Early America*. New York: Harper & Row, 1988.

Hill, Francis. *A Delusion of Satan: The Full Story of the Salem Witch Trials*. Cambridge: Da Capo Press, 1997.

Norton, Mary Beth. *In the Devil's Snare: The Salem Witchcraft Crisis of 1692*. New York: Vintage Books, 2002.

Several websites have interesting material and can refer you to actual accounts of the trials. To investigate: www.law.umkc.edu/faculty/projects/ftrials/salem/salem.htm